Till's Christmas

12/94

Merry Christmas!

Love,

Mrs. Toombs

Till's Christmas

Nola Thacker

AN
APPLE
PAPERBACK

SCHOLASTIC INC.
New York Toronto London Auckland Sydney

No part of this publication may be reproduced in whole or in part, or stored in a retrieval system, or transmitted in any form or by any means, electronic, mechanical, photocopying, recording, or otherwise, without written permission of the publisher. For information regarding permission, write to Scholastic Inc., 730 Broadway, New York, NY 10003.

ISBN 0-590-43543-4

12 11 10 9 8 7 6 5 4 3   4 5 6 7/9

Printed in the U.S.A.   40

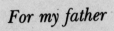

For my father

Contents

1

Over the River
and Through the Woods

"Matilda?"

Till Wyndham didn't look up. She knew if she did, she'd see her Aunt Lenore, who was sitting next to her Aunt Clare. Aunt Clare, looking deceptively small, her eyes half-shut but unblinking, would be pressed into the corner of the left wing chair, her hands wrapped around a mug of tea. Overflowing the other wing chair, swathed in a skirt and jacket that made her look deceptively large, Aunt Lenore was smiling and fluttering her fingers and looking wide-eyed delighted to see

Till. As if she doesn't see me all the time, Till said to herself.

"Matilda!"

"Who invited all these tacky people," muttered Till. She concentrated on the stack of dishes and crumpled napkins she was collecting as she made her way around the living room. At an end table she went into a deep knee bend, leaned slightly back, and scooped up another cake plate. In her mind she saw a row of judges holding up placards. An announcer's voice was saying, "Yes, ladies and gentlemen, it looks like Till Wyndham's score is going to be a perfect ten. But wait . . . we still don't have a score from the Soviet judge. No, he's raising his card. It looks like . . ."

"Matilda?"

Surrendering, Till straightened up. "Coming."

She plowed her way through the disjointed, end-of-Thanksgiving Day bits of conversation being scattered around the room like cake crumbs. Variations on the Turkey theme, thought Till. Gobble, gobble.

"Here you go, sugar," said Aunt Lenore, holding out a plate as if it were a gift.

"Gee, thanks," said Till, but Aunt Lenore just smiled.

"You're welcome, sweetie. You are doing *so* much work. Better than a waitress, too, the way you handled those dishes. I remember, when I was doing work study at college? My job was in the cafeteria, and the first year it was busing tables. I tell you . . ."

Till suddenly felt an itch beneath her left shoulder blade. The announcer's voice started in her head again: "This is it, ladies and gentlemen. The over-the-shoulder scratch, while fully laden. She's positioning her weights. Can she make the reach? Will she be able to maintain her . . ."

Aunt Lenore's voice interrupted again. "Till? Now, you just let me know if there's anything I can do to help."

"Okay. Scratch my shoulder," said Till.

"W-what?"

"My shoulder," said Till. "It itches. I can't reach it . . . oh, never mind. No, there's nothing you can do. You're a guest. I just live here."

The moment the words flew out of her mouth, Till was sorry she'd said them. She watched her aunt's weather-brown face pucker, then smooth out to expressionlessness.

Say something back, she willed her aunt. But of course, Aunt Lenore didn't. She never did. Now she directed a smile at Till, not quite looking into Till's face, and stood up. "Excuse me for just a minute," she murmured and hurried into the middle of the living room, stopping for a moment, as if she were lost, before going over to the group gathered on the sofa around Till's baby brother, Peter.

Till looked down over her armload of dishes

into her Aunt Clare's dark brown eyes. They were not friendly eyes.

"Well."

"Uh, well," said Till.

"Isn't it wonderful how, if a person feels bad, they can make other people feel bad, too?"

"Uh . . . no . . ."

"No?"

"Uh, can I get you anything?"

"Till, how thoughtful of you." Her aunt's voice, in contrast to Aunt Lenore's cheerful breathless staccato, was at the best of times an edgy drawl. Now it was drawn out thin and low, a sliding sort of growl. "Since I'm a guest, I think I'll have another piece of coconut cake. Here you go, Matilda." Aunt Clare uncrossed her arms, picked up her plate and fork, and set them down with unnecessary firmness on top of the stack Till was holding.

Till staggered back and teetered around like a juggler, barely keeping her balance beneath the load. Then, mortified and fuming, she swung around beneath the dangerously wobbling stack and made her shaky way quickly back to the kitchen. She didn't breathe once. Only when she had set the dirty dishes down hard by the sink, where they began to slide every which way, did she let go. "Hnnnh!"

"Hey!" said her brother Samuel, who'd been

put in charge of loading and unloading the dish-washer for the day.

"Is for horses," snapped Till. She turned to the three-layer coconut-lemon cake on the counter and picked up the cake knife. "Prepare to meet thy maker," she told the cake.

"*Mom* made the cake," said Sammy. "And besides, that's sacrilegious."

"Give me a *break*." Till raised the knife — and stopped. Then, almost of its own accord the knife moved over, sliced down, and Till was sliding an enormous chunk of cake onto her aunt's plate. Let her eat cake, then, thought Till spitefully.

"Wow," said Annabel, coming into the kitchen with more plates. "Leave some for me. Who's that for?"

"Aunt Clare." Till gave her little sister a cannibal smile. Annabel stepped hastily back. Holding the single plate aloft, Till pushed her way back through the dining room and into the living room to stand in front of her aunt.

"Here," she said, much more loudly and firmly than even she had intended.

A small hush began to spread among everyone nearby.

Aunt Lenore and the relatives on the sofa paused in their solemn coochie-cooing of Peter.

Till's mother stopped in the hall doorway.

Till stared down once more into Aunt Clare's

sharp brown eyes. They had an amused, knowing expression now, the suffering-fools-gladly-when-they're-entertaining look, she'd say it was. She looked at Till, looked at the enormous chunk of cake Till was holding trophy-high, looked back at Till.

Till felt herself go red-hot with mortal embarrassment. Instinctively, she jerked both hands up to cover her face, forgetting, for one fatal moment, the cake.

The plate tilted back. The cake slid toward Till. She lurched forward.

The cake lifted up in a perfect arc, hung suspended for one endless moment, then broke into three separate layers and assorted pieces and rained down on Aunt Clare.

From the den, where her grandparents and her father were watching the football game, she heard her grandmother cry, "Reverse hallelujah! That should've been a touchdown!"

Aunt Clare said, "I think it was!" She started to laugh. Suddenly a wave of laughter flooded the room, followed by a second wave from the dining room, as everyone poked forward to see what had happened. Till's relatives by blood and relatives by marriage, by courtesy and by long association, her whole family, was laughing. At her.

"No!" cried Till. "Stop it. Stop laughing!" Still holding the plate, she pushed her way out of the room. She charged through the kitchen, dropped the plate with an ominous crack on the kitchen table, snatched a coat off the hook, and fled the house.

The town of Evergreen, wrapped in gray and cold and sodden fallen leaves, was Sunday silent as Till ran through it, clutching her mother's old navy pea jacket around her shoulders. "Like an orphan," she thought. She hurried past curbs full of parked cars, in front of houses full of people in various stages of Thanksgiving. Each house seemed more enviably normal and calm than the next, and it made her feel even worse.

"I didn't mean to do it," Till said, passing the Flomaton house, gleaming like a wedding cake on the corner.

"It was an accident," she said, cutting across the vacant lot behind the Texaco station.

"It *was*." She stopped on the bridge above the railroad tracks, which bisected the town a little further up. She turned her back to it, facing down the tunnel of trees that lined the edge of the track bed. On days that weren't gray, she could see all the way to the end of the line, to where the sun came up, or so it seemed. On days that weren't so gray, she could imagine herself, elegant as in an old movie, going down those same tracks. She would be sitting in a window seat, watching the whole familiar world slide by, waiting until the landscape started to change. Till could see it now. . . .

"Excuse me." The mousy little person in the seat across the aisle leaned toward her. Till looked up from the book she was reading and peered inquiringly at the person who'd interrupted her. "Well," said the person. "I just wondered. Weren't you a cheerleader at Julia Tutwiler High? In Evergreen?"

Till smiled in a kindly, superior way. "No. Why do you ask?"

"Well, you are so beautiful, and coordinated. I couldn't help but notice, when you were walking down the aisle, that you didn't even lose your balance when we went around the worst curves."

"A cheerleader." Till shrugged. "No, being a cheerleader never interested me. It's so — limiting."

"An athlete then? Soccer? Track!"

"I did set some state track records. I believe they still stand . . . of course, some people do burn out early that way," said Till. "I didn't . . ."

"Ha!" said Till. "Double tacky ha."

There's been some mistake, she thought. When they handed out lives, they got mine mixed up with some donkey's or something.

"Sure," she answered herself. "And all it takes

is someone to come along and give your old donkey frog self a kiss and you'll be turned into a princess." Hard on the heels of frogs and prince's kisses came thoughts of ugly ducklings and swans, but she put them firmly aside.

I'm trapped, she thought, looking down at the crossties. What am I going to do?

I could ask someone.

She frowned. Her mother would make a speech full of love and loving and brisk boosting-up. Her father would call her a pet name, probably — Till closed her eyes briefly — Puddinghead, offer her a trip to the Dairy Queen, or, worst of all, perhaps launch into a serious talk.

"Great," said Till.

Then there was Aunt Clare, who might really have an idea or an answer. Aunt Clare never seemed to try to be helpful or particularly friendly, but when she asked Till questions, she listened to the answers. And she gave good presents.

But now she couldn't ask her Aunt Clare anything. What is wrong with me, thought Till, and saw the cake sail through the air toward her aunt, a perfect slam dunk shot.

The faraway whistle of a train jerked her mind back to the bridge. The tunnel of bare trees and evergreens that lined the track had begun to take on the color of the night that was falling, familiar, faintly melancholy, a little spooky.

Till straightened. "No use crying," she said. "No use crying over spilt cake."

People would be leaving. Thanksgiving was almost over.

She turned and headed for home.

2

Tidings of Comfort and Joy

Mrs. Wyndham laughed.

"Mom?" said Annabel.

"Suse?" said Mr. Wyndham.

"Oh, I can't wait," Susannah Wyndham said into the telephone. She wound the cord around her free hand, and with the receiver pressed to her ear, walked into the hall, closing the door behind her.

"Who was *that*?" Annabel asked Samuel, who'd answered the phone.

Samuel shrugged. "Some lady."

Annabel headed for the door.

"Annabel."

Annabel stopped and looked at her father inquiringly.

"Where are you going?"

"To listen and see what's going on," Annabel answered patiently.

"No."

"Why not?"

"Really, Annabel," said Till. "It's extremely tacky to eavesdrop. Extremely."

"Judge not that you be not judged," said Samuel, suddenly coming down on his eight-year-old sister's side.

"Yeah," said Annabel. "*A*-men." She went off into a gale of giggles.

Their father cleared his throat. "Matilda is right. . . ."

Since her father was agreeing with her, Till decided that she could tolerate his use of her whole name, this once.

". . . But for all the wrong reasons."

"What!" Till said.

"See," said Samuel.

"It *is* too tacky to eavesdrop," Till said.

"I was thinking more along the lines of ill-mannered and rude," her father answered.

"Well, how'm I going to find out, then?" asked Annabel, getting to the heart of the matter.

Till turned on Annabel. "Who said you had a right to know, spyface, pieface?"

"I don't have a pieface! And how come I can't be a spy?"

"Why don't we finish cleaning up the kitchen here, and let your mother tell us what is going on when she comes back," said Mr. Wyndham. "*If* she feels like it."

"She might not feel like coming back?" asked Annabel.

"She might not feel like *telling* us, Annabel," said Till.

"Oh. I can't even ask her, Daddy?"

"No," her father said.

A crash made them all jump. Till knew what had happened without even turning around. "You were trying to juggle plates, weren't you, Sammy?"

"No! Only just one coffee cup."

"You're going to get it," said Till. "Wait'll Mom gets off the phone."

"Unless you're perfect, don't cast the first stone!"

"I'm not casting stones, you're casting dishes!"

"Better than cake!" Sam gave a hoot.

"Oh, yeah? How'd you like to be turned into a bunch of loaves and fishes, Samuel!"

"Stop!" Mr. Wyndham held his dish towel up like a truce flag — or, maybe, thought Till, more like the last lap signal on the Indy 500. "Next time, Samuel, use potatoes to juggle. Let us have no more mention of cakes. And, meanwhile, all of you, clean up the mess."

"Oh, goody, we're sharing. Big points in heaven, right Sam?" Till glared at her brother, who glared back.

Then more laughter, a long, throaty chuckle unlike any sound Till could ever remember her mother uttering, echoed from the vicinity of the gossip bench in the hall.

Everyone in the kitchen froze.

Then Annabel said, "I don't think it counts that you broke a cup, Samuel."

They finished cleaning the kitchen. But no one would make a move to go. Till wiped off the front of the cabinets. Samuel straightened the chairs around the kitchen table. Mr. Wyndham made a show of folding the dish towel just right. Annabel just stared at the door.

Suddenly Mrs. Wyndham pushed it open and just stood there, beaming at them. "Look how clean the kitchen is!"

"I broke a cup," said Samuel.

"Mama, who was on the phone?" asked Annabel.

"Oh, those old dishes. Don't worry, kiddo. . . . Well, I've some things to do. . . ." She trailed out of the kitchen, leaving everyone staring after her.

"Are *you* going to ask her, Daddy?"

"Hmmm? No. No, of course not, Annabel."

"Well, somebody had better," said Annabel grimly. "Mama's acting weird."

Till, watching her father slowly finish wiping out the cast-iron frying pan and put it back in the side oven, thought, "She's not acting weird, she's acting like someone else."

Till was huddled against the side of her school, trying to soak up the last bit of warmth from the half-hearted sunshine as recess raged around her.

Lulinda Harris, who was standing nearby, surveying everyone like a queen reviewing her subjects, said, "I'm going out for junior varsity next year."

"Me, too," chimed Melanie Mack, Lulinda's best friend for the week. "Are you going to wear blue and orange, Lulinda?"

"You'd better start practicing, then," said Sarie Knudson. She was standing on one foot, doing ankle rotations with the other. Sarie hardly ever just stood still.

"Don't you know anything, Sarie? Practice doesn't start until April. *Next* April." Melanie tossed her head, then reached up quickly to make sure the silver initial barrette holding her thick black hair back on one side had not come loose.

"Good thing it wasn't last April," Sarie said. "Or you'd have already missed it. And you'll never make cheerleader, anyway, Watermelanie, if you keep fussing with your hair."

"Don't call me that!" Melanie tossed her head again, reached instinctively for her hair, then yanked her hand down.

"AND you'd better be glad I'm not trying out. I can do backflips."

Lulinda focused on Sarie for an instant. "You'd better be nice, Sarie. Or I won't come cheer your soccer games."

"You have to. It's the rule." Sarie knew how to get the last word and didn't mind doing it. It was one of the reasons, thought Till, that so many people preferred to get along with her. If Lulinda was the school royalty, Sarie was the general.

I guess that makes me and Melanie the subjects. Or the troops, she thought glumly. She didn't like the idea of being lumped with Melanie, even in her own mind.

Lulinda smiled suddenly, and reached up and smoothed back her own blonde hair as if she were petting a kitten. Till followed the direction of her gaze to where some of the sixth-grade boys were playing football.

Melanie did too. "Gross!" she cried. "Aren't they, Lulinda?"

Lulinda didn't answer.

"I'm getting my ears pierced for Christmas, Lulinda," announced Melanie.

Lulinda half turned her head.

"We're going into Birmingham to shop, and

I'm going to get it done at Loveman's. At the jewelry counter. And I get to pick out any pair of earrings I want."

"They have to be at least fourteen karat gold-filled," said Lulinda, giving the matter her full attention now. "Otherwise you might get an infection in your earlobes."

"I expect they'll be solid gold," said Melanie airily.

"You're so lucky," said Lulinda. "*My* mother won't let me get my ears pierced until I'm fourteen." But the way she said it made it sound as if Melanie's mother was committing an indiscretion, letting her only daughter get her ears pierced so young. Melanie's fair skin colored, faintly, but she was prettier than she was quick. The way she looked around, Till could tell she was trying to think how to answer.

Sarie, on whom such sneak attacks were wasted, said, "You can't wear earrings when you play soccer. Someone might yank them right off your ears. Just rip 'em off."

"Sarie!" Melanie's voice was piercing.

Till laughed.

"Sarie, you are so gross," said Melanie furiously. "And who asked you anything, Till? What are you laughing at? Bloody, gross earlobes are funny?"

"Melanie, please!" Lulinda clapped her hands

over her own ears, shaking her head.

"Oh! I'm sorry," said Melanie, glaring at Sarie and Till.

"What does your being sorry have to do with it?" asked Sarie, laughing.

"You are so immature!" Melanie's pale skin had gone from faintly pink to mottled red.

Their teacher, Ms. Jungwirth, had come out on the steps. She raised her whistle and began to blow it, signaling the end of recess.

Lulinda had taken her hands down from her ears. "She's so bossy."

"Napoleon complex," said Sarie.

"No kidding," said Till. "Big time."

"What's a Napoleon complex?" asked Lulinda.

Till waited for Sarie to explain, but Sarie didn't say anything.

"Till?" said Melanie, smiling. "Tell us, Till."

"Sarie knows," said Till.

Sarie shrugged.

"It's, uh, it means that, uh, Ms. Jungwirth is like Napoleon."

"Why?" asked Melanie.

"Why? Don't you know? If you don't know, I'm not going to tell you," said Till desperately.

"You don't know, do you?" asked Melanie. "You lied. You just pretended you knew."

"I did not! And what difference does it make?"

"It just means she's short, and that makes her want to rule the world, basically," said Sarie at

18

last. "Napoleon was short, see, and that's why they say he set out to conquer the world."

"I knew that," said Till.

"Sure." Melanie smiled nastily. "Sure you did."

The three girls started toward the steps. Till trailed after them, hating herself for it.

"What are you getting for Christmas, Lulinda?" asked Melanie.

"I might get my ears pierced," Till blurted out.

Melanie looked over her shoulder. "You and what army? Napoleon's?" She laughed loudly. It was no consolation that Sarie and Lulinda didn't join in.

Till stopped. Everyone else kept walking. Why did I do that? she thought. Why, why, why?

She stayed still for a minute, then walked slowly back to class. She was sitting at her desk, her eyes still burning, her mind still replaying the conversation, when she suddenly realized just how stupid she was. She groaned. Orange and blue were the junior high colors, and how had everyone known about trying out for cheerleading and what to wear? Everyone — except her.

"In here!" her mother called out that afternoon as Till banged through the front door. Till went into the dining room and found her mother and her aunt Clare sitting cross-legged on the floor next to the china cabinet, with a large book balanced on their knees between them.

19

"Oh," said Till. She hadn't seen her aunt since Thanksgiving, and a couple of weeks might not have been long enough to forget about the cake attack.

"Oh," said her aunt.

Till looked at the two of them. They had an air of conspiracy.

"Were you talking about me?" said Till.

"Not yet," said her aunt. "But if you'll leave the room . . ."

Till suddenly grinned. "No way. What are y'all doing?"

"How was school, Tillie?" asked her mom. "Did you learn anything?"

"Tillie?" said her aunt Clare.

"Mom, it's Till."

"Better." Aunt Clare nodded.

Till hesitated. "School was fine."

"But of course you didn't learn anything," put in her aunt.

"At school?" asked Till.

Her aunt started to laugh. "I'm leaving," she said, and stood up in a quick, single motion that reminded Till of Sarie going up to head a soccer ball at school. "See ya, Till," she said. She held her hand up to her ear like a phone receiver and said to Till's mother, "Later."

"Mom," repeated Till as her aunt charged out, "what are you doing?"

Her mother shrugged. "Something we old people do. Something I swore I would never do to *my* children." She raised the book so that Till could see gold lettering on the spine.

"*The Cavalier*," Till read aloud. "What is it?"

"My high school yearbook in all its glory. Senior year."

Mrs. Wyndham paused.

"Oh," said Till, noncommittally.

"I promised myself I'd never get it out and make my children listen to the stories of the good old days. Such as they were." She made an elaborate show of closing the yearbook.

"Oh," said Till again, and then, because she really was sort of interested in spite of herself, added, "wait."

Till knelt down next to her mother, who flipped the book open again to a long row of small black-and-white photographs and pointed to the lower right-hand corner of the page. "Me."

Till studied the photograph.

"You look sort of the same."

"Nah," said her mother. She made a face. "I do not have teased hair, for one thing. And I'd *never* wear earrings like that again." She turned the pages over and pointed to another picture, this one in the middle of the page. Till bent over and read the tiny print beneath.

"Leah Frances."

"My best friend."

"Oh, yeah. I guess you've talked about her before."

What else could Till say besides that? I don't have any friends, she thought, remembering the day that had just passed, possibly the worst day of her entire life to date. Not that I care, she added to herself.

Her mother went on. "We moved every year when I was growing up. Daddy just liked to travel. He was a newspaperman of all trades, could even set hot type — no one does that anymore, it's all done by computer now — but back then, you could always get a job anywhere, knowing how to do that. . . ."

Till knew this part of the story. Her grandparents had traveled until her grandfather died on board a train, still headed somewhere. Her grandmother had come to stay with them, right before Till was born, and died when Till was still a baby. Till didn't think she could remember her grandmother at all. But she felt like she still had plenty of relatives on her father's side, there in Evergreen. More than enough, in her opinion. Abruptly her thoughts switched back to her mother's story.

"Anyway, my junior year, we moved again. But this time, we stayed for two years. I finished high school, made real friends. Leah was my best friend."

"I'm not going to have a best friend until college," said Till. "When I meet interesting people. What I mean is, I'm sure Leah was really interesting. . . ."

"She thought I was," said Mrs. Wyndham. "I'd traveled, lived in all sorts of places. She'd grown up in the same place all her life. She thought I was exotic!"

"Well, no wonder. Look at me. I've had to grow up in the same place all my life. It's boring. I mean, who wants to be friends with people you've known your whole life. Shallow, stupid people who laugh at you!"

"And then we went to the university together, and after the first year, Leah takes off for New York. By herself. Who was exotic then? . . ."

"I'm going to college in New York, and have a best friend then. Someone interesting!"

"Oh, maybe you won't have to wait *that* long." Till's mother closed the yearbook and put it back into the linen drawer at the bottom of the china cabinet. "That was her, Leah, on the phone Thursday night. And this came today. It's all settled."

Scrambling to her feet, Mrs. Wyndham took an envelope off the dining room sideboard. She held it out as Till stood up. The name Susannah Skinner Wyndham with no Ms. or even Mrs. danced before Till's eyes. Then, from the jumble of spikey black letters, two words leapt out: New York.

23

Mrs. Wyndham said, "She's coming. They're coming from New York City. For Christmas. Leah, her husband, and their daughter. We're going to have a really, really special Christmas this year! And Deirdre, that's Leah's daughter, and she's in sixth grade, too, like you, is getting out of school the week before Christmas, and she's coming down first. So, you see, you may not have to wait so long to have an interesting best friend after all!"

Not until later, when Annabel pointed out that they'd never had company for Christmas, just family, not until later, when Mrs. Wyndham said something about it being the best Christmas yet and Mr. Wyndham said, "Let's wait and see," not until later, when Till realized that her mother had suggested something completely disgusting and corny, the possibility that she become best friends with the daughter of her mother's best friend, did Till see the other problems, hidden away, layer on layer, like the pungent skins of an onion.

But at that moment, looking at the envelope and her mother's shining green eyes and her big-toothed grin so like the joyous grin in the year-book, and feeling, suddenly, the whole weight of the building block-looking old brick house, the whole weight of the whole square and not par-ticularly historic or famous or interesting for any reason town she lived in, Till could think of only one question.

She looked at her mother in horror, her own green eyes squinching like Peter's when he was thinking about howling. "Mother!" she cried. "From New York the city? Here? No! What am I going to do?"

3

Bah and Humbug

"Hush," said Till to Peter, "and I'll tell you the story of how I was adopted."

Peter smacked his lips, staring at the soft sculpture mobile over his head.

"Take my word for it, the taste would disappoint you," said Till. "Now, are you listening? Listen.

"I am adopted, you know. That explains how I got put in with all these slow, skinny, rootbound people in our — your — family. Like those ferns Mom keeps hanging on the front porch, only happy if their roots are all mashed together in a little bitty pot, and no use for the sun or traveling or anything. And look at me. You call this slow and skinny?" She pulled her shirt tight across her chest. "I'm just about to turn twelve and I'm already getting a profile. Next thing you know it'll be all that other stuff."

"Babby," said Peter.

"You don't know about that yet," Till added hastily. "But still. Mom said it didn't happen to her until she was sixteen. So it just proves it. What I said. I'm adopted.

"You're not. You . . . you are, I am sorry to say, definitely blood of their blood, flesh of their flesh, bone of their bone. . . ."

Unimpressed by her biblical rhythms, Peter let his eyelids droop slightly.

Till rolled on in a style of which Sammy would have approved. "You are begat of a begat, but I am a stranger, of other peoples, other tribes. Lo, my world is an alien one, my story sad. Hear, O Peter . . .

"Are you listening? I'm adopted, I tell you. And you're not. But there is hope for you yet. Stick with me, kid. . . ."

Peter's eyes closed, and his mouth fell open in a small snuffling snore.

"Fine. Sleep. See if I care." Till jerked a blanket up over her baby brother and went into the den. She picked up the remote of the TV and began to punch the buttons. The stations flipped silently by. From the corner of her eye she could see the satellite dish swiveling outside the den window, like a demented dinosaur-sized flower.

"Bah," said Till as a colorized version of Natalie Wood in *Miracle on 34th Street* popped into view.

No matter where she turned, Christmas was in the air, from the Christmas tree in front of the courthouse, to the red and green construction paper decorations in the hall at school. Only at her house was she safe from Christmas, and that was just a matter of time. Her mother was "saving" all the usual Christmas activities for Deirdre Frances's arrival.

Till groaned. She could just envision a girl from New York, a girl who would make Lulinda and Melanie and Sarie rolled into one look dim and uninteresting, decking the Wyndham home with boughs of holly — not to mention homemade Christmas decorations. And that was just the beginning.

"Although it might as well be the end," muttered Till. A large man in an elf suit began to wave his hands on the screen, selling something for Christmas to the tune of tinny Christmas carols. "Bah," said Till again. "Bah and good-*bye*!"

She clicked off the television, raised her feet, put the control between them, and lowered it carefully down onto the end table. The den grew dim and still. Till closed her eyes wearily. What, after all, was there to see?

She tried instead to concentrate, to come up with an idea that would prevent the Christmas disaster ahead. She tried to imagine a perfect Christmas.

A scene from one of Laura Ingalls Wilder's books flashed into her mind, and for a moment she conjured up herself, smiling gently at the newcomer, this Deirdre, letting this Deirdre see that here, in her family, in her town, Christmas was a simple, honest affair in the true American tradition of the pioneers.

Then she imagined Annabel being told that an orange was one of her big Christmas presents that year.

"Get real," said Till aloud.

She raised her arm and pressed the back of her wrist against her forehead, wishing as she did so that she could see how she looked doing that. Then she imagined herself, leaning languidly back on a velvet sofa, directing an indistinct but handsome sort in the fine art of draping strings of real pearls up and down the exquisite Christmas tree glittering in her townhouse window.

"Like the popcorn strings I had as a child," she murmured. But it didn't work. She groaned.

The overhead light snapped on. Controlling her impulse to jump, Till opened her eyes.

"I'm home," said her mother.

"Yes," said Till.

"Are you all right?"

Till groaned again and let her arm drop over the edge of the sofa. Mrs. Wyndham came over and put her hand on her daughter's forehead. Half-liking the attention, Till pulled back. "I'm not a baby," she said.

Her mother pulled back, too. "I hope you're not coming down with something, right now, before the holidays."

Till thought for a moment. The idea tempted her. She could retreat into her room, safely away from all those maddening things her family insisted on doing as part of the Christmas season, safe from the New Yorkers, safe from it all. But no. If a thing is worth doing, it's worth doing well, her mother had said probably a million times. And to be sick at Christmas right now meant she'd have to go to bed immediately and stay there until the New Year. Even if she wanted to, she didn't think she could fool her mother into letting her stay in bed that long.

"I'm fine," said Till. "Just fine."

"Good," said Mrs. Wyndham. "Is Peter . . ."

"He's asleep. Mom?"

"Hmm?"

"If you could have anything that you wanted for Christmas, what would you want?"

"That's easy. I already have what I want. My family, my friends, my work."

Till sighed. She might have known her mother

would answer like that. "Not even a million dollars?"

"I'd take the million if it was offered. My mother didn't raise no dummies."

Till waited. Finally her mother said, "What would you like?"

"A perfect Christmas. That's what I want for Christmas."

"Oh, Till. What a nice thought." Before Till could continue, her mother was leaning over and kissing her on the forehead. "We'll have a wonderful Christmas. Really special."

Before Till could explain that she hadn't meant exactly what her mother thought she meant (she thought), her mother went on.

"You know, I am so excited about seeing Leah again. It's been ages. But I'm a little nervous, too. What if we've changed? I don't *think* we have. What I mean is, we've stayed in touch, we still write, talk on the phone, not as much as we used to, but still, when we do, it feels just like it always does. But it's not the same, is it?"

"Mom."

"I know. I'm being silly. Not to mention incoherent. It'll be fine. A perfect Christmas." Till's mother patted Till's arm. Till's throat suddenly tightened. I have to face the facts, she thought. There's no such thing as Santa Claus. And even if there was, a perfect Christmas just doesn't get dropped down the chimney.

If a thing's worth doing . . . Till jolted up.

She wasn't going to give up. Her mother wanted a perfect Christmas just as much as she did. They both wanted the same thing. But it was up to her, Till, to see that they got it.

Just hold that bah, thought Till. And add some humbug.

4

Deck the Halls

"He's Hot. He's Cool. He's . . . !!!"
"Find your BEST Colors."
"One Hundred Fabulous Ideas to Wrap Christmas Up Right."
"SPECIAL Christmas Issue!!!"

Till stood at the magazine rack at the Evergreen Pharmacy, trying to concentrate. But she felt as if she had earphones tuned into separate stations in each ear.

Honest to baby Jesus, thought Till. Or maybe even Jesus wept. Ever since Samuel had gotten religion at the Baptist church revival he had

33

gone to last summer, she'd taken up creative biblical descriptions. It made Sammy mad as fire.

Till smiled to herself, then brought her mind back to the job at hand.

"He's Hot. He's Cool."

She's from New York, thought Till. The farthest I've been is to Fort Walton Beach, Florida.

At least I've got a profile. Not like Lulinda's, but . . .

"You sure read a lot, don't you?"

Till blinked and half-turned her head. As if she'd been summoned by Till's thoughts, Lulinda Harris was standing in the aisle in all her cool, hot perfection.

"Hi," said Till weakly. She'd been keeping a different kind of profile, a very low profile, since that humiliating incident at recess. No one seemed to have noticed. Not that I care, Till reminded herself quickly. But I wish she hadn't caught me reading, her thoughts hurried on. Especially this.

Lulinda reached out for *"He's Cool. He's Hot. He's . . . !!!"* studied it briefly, then wrinkled her nose and put it back. "I didn't know you read magazines."

Who cares? said the voice inside her. Who cares about Lulinda, always changing friends, as fickle as the weather. If I had a best friend, the voice said scornfully, I'd keep her.

"Sure," said Till. "A friend of mine is coming

to visit for Christmas. From New York. I thought I'd get some ideas for fixing up, I mean decorating, the house."

"Really? A guy?"

"No! No. An old friend. We've known each other since we were babies, but we haven't seen each other in years. Ages."

Lulinda studied Till. "A girlfriend? What's her name?"

"Deirdre. Deirdre Frances."

"New York City?"

"Where else?" Till smiled a little. "Of course, it'll be a very quiet visit. But I'm hoping she'll come to school one day. To meet everyone."

Lulinda studied Till for a moment longer, then seemed to lose interest. "Sure."

"I mean it," said Till.

"Sure," repeated Lulinda. "See ya."

Till frowned. "See ya," she said to Lulinda's back. And then she realized what was wrong. Lulinda hadn't believed her. She'd thought Till was lying.

Again, said a little voice inside.

Someday, Till answered the voice, someday she'll be sorry. She let her mind leap forward to the future, and saw herself, taller, with cleavage, and very famous for her brilliant mind: "Till!" An equally famous person was calling her name across the crowded, elegant party. She was turning to answer. Turning gracefully, pirouetting

35

perfectly . . . but what was this? How could she, Till, so famous she was known by only one name, how could she, such an elegant, beautiful, velvet-and-jewel-clad goddess, trip? And fall? And knock over an entire table of caviar and champagne???

Till shook her head, shaking the image loose. She reached out resolutely and picked up the *"SPECIAL Christmas Issue!!!"* and headed toward the cash register.

"A blue spruce," repeated Till encouragingly.

Her father, reclined in his recliner in front of the fireplace, not doing much of anything, said, "A pretty tree. Not native to these parts, I believe."

"You can buy them. Or a Douglas fir. They're very popular. And they're from the South. Not Alabama, but the South."

"Don't worry, Tillie. We'll get the tree in plenty of time. Your mother — and I — just thought we'd wait until Deirdre gets here."

"Daddy! You're not listening." Till felt her voice thin up dangerously close to a whine and stopped. Then she spoke softly, carefully. "Of course, it's a wonderful idea to wait. I'm glad we are . . ."

"That's the spirit." Her father slid a little further down in his recliner.

"But we don't want to make Deirdre go out and hike all over the woods looking for a plain old tree, do we? After all, she's coming all the way from New York. She's probably used to real trees, really special ones. We should get one she'll feel right at home with."

Her father didn't say anything. Till plunged on. "And we could decorate a special tree right."

"Right?"

Till unrolled the magazine, which she'd studied carefully all afternoon, and flipped it open. "Look. Like this. See? You can flock the branches. You know, put artificial snow on them, and then tie silver bows on each branch tip, with gold satin balls in between. Isn't it elegant?"

"Elegant? Well . . . I've always sort of liked red and green for Christmas. And all the ornaments we've made."

"Tacky," moaned Till. Seeing her father's expression, she hastily said, "Well, not exactly tacky."

"Till. We'll pick out a beautiful tree. We'll make new, elegant decorations. Your mother is planning a very special Christmas. And you know, traditions appeal to a lot of people. I bet Deirdre and her family will like all our traditions just fine."

"You don't understand!" cried Till.

"Understand what? Do you think people in New York put their pants on any different? Maybe hang them across the room and take a running leap and jump in? They're just people. If they spoke a different language, even, you can still smile and be understood."

"Well, I can't just stand around smiling all Christmas long, can I? And when have you ever been to New York?"

"Never. Okay. And it doesn't show, does it?"

"Are you going to tell me not to judge a book by the cover now?" said Till disgustedly.

Her father thought a minute. "No. No, but you have to know how to look at the cover, don't you?"

"Huh!"

"Your aunt Clare's been. She lived there for a while."

"Aunt Clare? New York?"

"Yep. Thought you could tell by looking. . . ."

"This is not funny!" Till rolled the magazine up and clutched it against her chest with both hands. "She . . . they'll come down here and laugh at us. And we'll deserve it, too!"

Ignoring the odd expression that suddenly appeared on her father's face, Till turned and left with as much dignity as she could muster.

She wasn't giving up.

That night before bed, she followed her mother to Peter's room. Peter was asleep. Susannah Wyndham was leaning against Peter's crib.

"I don't know why people say 'sleeping like babies,' " said Mrs. Wyndham as Till came in. She reached down and pushed Peter's left foot back under his blanket. Peter slept on, indifferent, determined.

"He's not sleeping like a baby. He's sleeping like a night nurse after a double shift, like a Saint Bernard after a hard day in the Alps, like a, like a. . . ."

"Salesperson during the Christmas rush," Till supplied.

"Exactly," said her mother.

"Mom. About Christmas."

"Uh-huh?"

"About making it really special this year, like you said. To make Deirdre and her parents feel welcome?"

"That's the idea." Her mother was still meditating on Peter.

Till opened her magazine and riffled through the pages noisily, until she got to the photograph of the gold and silver, white-flocked blue spruce. "Isn't this great? And look."

She paused.

At last her mother looked up. Till pointed to the picture of a banister festooned with ribbon and holly. "And look at this wreath. You can order it. It's made from genuine Christmas herbs. They're all 'symbolic of Christmas.' "

"I see there's a recipe for roast goose, too."

"It's *much* more traditional. Traditions are important, you know. There are plenty of them in here, too, for us to try." She handed the magazine to her mother, who fluttered the pages.

"Quite an assortment," her mother murmured. "Very thorough."

"Oh, yes," agreed Till. "But you can just pick the best ones."

"More than enough to keep a housewife, say, good and busy."

"I'll help," said Till. "We all will. You want it to be a really great Christmas, don't you?"

"Special. I do have an extraspecial Christmas in mind." Her mother smiled. "When I was growing up, we never knew where we were going to spend Christmas. Dad might have taken a job somewhere and forgotten to tell us about it and then, surprise, one day we were packing and the next day we were on the road. . . ."

"Keep the magazine as long as you want," Till said.

"Thank you, honey." She reached over and turned off the lamp. "Remember making this lamp for Peter? You and Annabel and Samuel?"

Till looked at the fat little ginger jar lamp, the base of which was plastered with drawings and magazine pictures, and then shellacked over. Samuel had chosen dinosaurs and monsters. "Monsters are animals, too," he had insisted. Annabel had been relentless about dogs. Till had chosen geese and ducks and one very long, thin cat, stretched halfway around the very bottom.

"A masterpiece," said Till, embarrassed by the lamp now.

Her mother stopped, framed by the light from the hall. "Yes. Yes . . . you never know when a masterpiece will turn up. Do you?"

5

Auld Acquaintance

Iron cold blanketed the entire world. The wind whined from north to south with an irritating, self-pitying sort of sound. Christmas isn't in the air, thought Till crossly, staring out of her bedroom window, but winter is.

The day of Deirdre's arrival had come. It was a school day — a week of school days still left before Christmas vacation — but they were all taking the day off to drive to the Birmingham airport.

"It's not fair," said Till aloud, "to have all this cold and not a bit of snow."

"Till? Are you ready?" Annabel, red with importance and excitement, thrummed on the doorframe of Till's room.

"Why are you doing that?" Till turned, still frowning. "The door is open."

"You said never come into your room without knocking."

"You are *so* literal-minded, Annabel."

"What's literal?" Annabel kept hovering in the door.

"It's what you are. . . . Well, come in, then."

Annabel stayed where she was. "You should come out. It's time."

"Time?"

"Time to go. To the airport. To get Deirdre!"

"Oh? Oh, of course. I'd *quite* let it slip my mind. Just let me get my coat. . . ."

"Till?"

"Hmmm?" Till brushed past Annabel, who thumped hurriedly after her.

"Till, is that all you're wearing?"

"What's wrong with what I'm wearing?"

"It's so . . . I mean, those are your cut-the-grass jeans!"

"Jeans and a sweatshirt are what I have on. That'll just have to do." Till kept walking.

"But . . ."

Literal *and* nosy.

"But . . ."

"Annabel."

43

"Okay," said Annabel. "But I don't think Mom's gonna like it."

"I'm old enough to make my own decisions about what I wear. As an eight-year-old, you couldn't be expected to understand."

"What's literal-minded?"

But Till hurried out the door, so she could have the last word.

Nothing in Till's closet was right for the occasion. Nothing, thought Till, in my whole life is right. At the last minute she had pulled on her oldest, most comfortable jeans.

Would her mother send her back inside? Till sat in the back left-hand corner of the car, where her mother couldn't see her in the rearview mirror. Her father wouldn't notice what she was wearing. Nor would Samuel nor, of course, Peter. For a moment, just as Till was sliding last into the car beside Annabel, she thought her mother was staring at her. But Mrs. Wyndham had only said, "I hope we don't overwhelm the poor kid."

Mr. Wyndham shook his head. "Susannah, she's from New York. It'll take more than a family of Wyndhams to shake her."

"Well, she is flying in by herself." Mrs. Wyndham started the car.

I've never even been *near* an airplane, thought Till, plunging into the injustice of it all. She didn't even notice that her father hadn't answered her mother, had turned to stare out the window.

* * *

The Birmingham airport didn't loom up suddenly. Nothing important or awesome about it, even if you had never actually seen an airport before, thought Till. "This is it?" she asked.

"How do the planes know where to go?" asked Annabel.

"They have men who are air-traffic controllers," said Samuel loftily.

"Girls can do that, too," said Annabel. "Can't they? What's an air-traffic controller?"

"It's a . . . you know. Everyone knows that."

"I don't," said Annabel.

Till felt a sudden rush of kinship with her younger sister. "They're traffic cops for planes. They stay in towers where they can see everything and talk to the pilots on earphones. Also they have radar," she explained.

Samuel rolled his eyes, big deal, then retreated into aloof silence. Till winked at Annabel.

But Annabel ruined it all. "What's literal?" she asked.

"Annabel!" muttered Till through clenched teeth.

"Literal?" asked their father.

"Literal-minded," said Annabel. "Till says I'm literal-minded, and she won't tell me what it means."

"It means you take everything seriously. At face value."

45

Annabel opened her mouth.

"It means you believe everything you're told, okay?" said Till.

"So?" said Annabel.

"Some things," began their father, but their mother was pulling up to a sign that read LOAD-ING AND UNLOADING ONLY/NO PARKING.

She parked the car and got out while their father slid over into the driver's seat for the trip back. "Wait here," she said.

"You don't want us to come with you, Suse?"

"Well . . . thanks, hon. But I think just Till."

"It's not fair," said Annabel. "Y'all get to see her first."

"Yes," said Mrs. Wyndham. "Ready, Till?"

Till grinned, forgetting to worry for just a moment. "I'm ready."

Mrs. Wyndham surveyed Till as she climbed out of the car.

Uh-oh, thought Till. But all her mother said was, "Beware of enterprises that require new clothes, eh? C'mon."

Till fell into step with her mother. "It's just a building, really," said Till. "The airport. Like an office."

"I guess it is. Other airports, the big hub ones, are probably sleeker."

"Yeah, I guess." Thinking of the airport as some sort of office building made it easier for Till to pretend this wasn't her first time in one. The

46

biggest surprise, really, was that it was so ordinary. Other airports are sleeker, she told herself.

Even the planes looked ordinary, maybe from her having seen them on television so much.

Passengers were just coming into the waiting area as Till and her mother got there.

"I didn't expect Deirdre's plane to make it on time!" exclaimed Mrs. Wyndham.

"How will you know who she is?"

Her mother smiled mysteriously. "I'll know by what she is wearing."

"You will?" Till looked down at her own clothes. If she'd known what Deirdre was going to be wearing, she might have worn something different. "How? Why didn't you . . ."

"There she is. Deirdre!"

Susannah Wyndham hurried forward, leaving Till feeling flat-footed and dumb. "Mother!"

But Mrs. Wyndham didn't hear. Till just had time to register that the girl toward whom her mother was heading was wearing a long, long red-and-green crocheted scarf exactly like the one Mrs. Wyndham had made for Till last Christmas. What a dumb scarf, Till had thought, and wore it only once, to keep from hurting her mother's feelings.

Then her mother was leaning slightly forward.

Till stared.

Mrs. Wyndham put her hands on the shoulders of the tall, graceful girl in the Christmas scarf, pressing her cheek to the girl's cheek, and kissing the air beside the girl's ear. Then the girl was doing the same thing back to Till's mother.

"I don't believe this," Till muttered. She clenched her teeth and marched forward.

" . . . this great scarf," Deirdre was saying. "What a *fabulous* idea!"

"Hello," Till said.

Deirdre turned. Till stuck out her hand. Deirdre looked down at it, then grasped it and leaned forward, as if she might be about to kiss the air by Till's cheek, too. Till let go of Deirdre's hand and stepped quickly back.

"This is Till. My oldest daughter."

"Of course! You're the first Till I've ever met."

"Oh. Well. Welcome. You're the first New Yorker I've ever met, I guess." Till smiled.

"And I was really born there," said Deirdre proudly.

What does that mean? thought Till. Mrs. Wyndham laughed, and said, "Come on, then. We'll get your luggage. You must be tired, taking such an early flight."

"A little, I guess. But you have to take early flights, especially this time of year. The traffic is so awful. You know." Now Deirdre smiled at Till.

"Traffic," repeated Till neutrally.

"The worst!" said Deirdre, as if she was agreeing with Till. "Mrs. Wyndham, I wanted to tell you how very much I appreciate your having me

48

for Christmas. It's so kind of you. And you, too, Till."

"We're glad to have you, dear. And how's your mother? Did she tell you we've been best friends since the Year One?"

Deirdre's laugh rang out. "You tell *me* about my mother. I want to hear all the stories about her."

Till trailed after her mother and Deirdre, who were talking easily, at top speed.

Expect the worst and be pleasantly surprised, she told herself.

I hate surprises.

I hate Christmas.

6

O Christmas Tree

"S o." Deirdre slid the last shirt over the hanger, buttoned the top button, smoothed the shirt front, then hung it carefully in the closet, precisely centered between two other hangers. "So. What's the story?"

"Story?"

"Yeah. You know. What's the setup, what're the plans? I mean, what have you been told about this gig?"

For one awful moment Till thought that Deirdre was speaking in tongues, and imagined having to call Samuel in to somehow interpret. She grinned.

"What's funny? Did they say something funny? About me?"

"Oh!" Now Till understood. "No. Mom just said you were coming to visit, you know. And you were coming early because you got out of school early. And your parents would be down Christmas Eve. And, uh, how, you know, she and your mother were best friends . . ."

"That's it? You're sure."

"Sure. Yes. That's it." Till was not going to mention the best-friend fantasy her mother had made up for Till and Deirdre, whole cloth — cloth she had, admittedly, embroidered a little herself. Deirdre already seemed like someone who didn't need a best friend, self-contained as a cat.

"So," said Deirdre impatiently. "What next?"

"Well, the plan is pretty basic," said Till. "This afternoon, we're going to get a Christmas tree."

"And?"

"And tonight, we'll start decorating it."

"That's it?"

"That's the plan. It takes awhile to get the tree, you know."

"They don't deliver?"

"Who?"

"The tree people."

"No. We're the tree people. We go and get the tree. Out in the woods."

"You mean we do a George Washington?"

"Huh? Oh. That's good." Till laughed. Deirdre didn't. "We do a George Washington, except, you know, it's a cedar tree, not a cherry tree."

"Well," said Deirdre. "I cannot tell a lie. I've never done anything like this before. I'm sure it will be *fascinating*."

"Really?"

"Really. When in Rome, you know."

"Do as the Romans do," said Till, relieved she knew that one.

"Listen, I'm going to take a nap. I'm beat."

"Don't you want any lunch?"

"No, I ate on the plane." Deirdre rolled her eyes. "You know where lunchroom food goes to die? They recycle it to the airlines for the tourist class." She flopped back on the bed and closed her eyes. "Or maybe it's the other way around. Wake me in time to change, okay?"

Till waited a moment longer, but Deirdre had apparently finished. "Okay," she whispered, and tiptoed out of her room.

"Did you hear the one about the lunatic in the woods?" asked Annabel.

"No," said Deirdre. "I didn't hear the one about the lunatic in the woods. Where are we, anyway?"

"In the woods," said Annabel.

"With lunatics," said Samuel.

"Speak for yourself," said Till.

"That is not funny," said Deirdre sharply.

Ahead, Till could see her father, with the baby carrier on his back, Peter bobbing along like the reverse figurehead on a ship. Farther ahead, in flashes, she could see the red of her mother's coat.

"We're almost there," Mrs. Wyndham called back.

Till wasn't sure, but she thought she heard her father snort.

"Are we lost?" demanded Deirdre.

"NO," said Till. "We are not lost. I told you. Mom's a timber cruiser for the lumber company."

"Whatever that means," said Deirdre.

"She looks at a bunch of trees they want to cut down and tells them how many feet of wood they have. And she marks the best trees for them to cut down. Like for telephone poles. Where do you think telephone poles come from?"

"I've never wondered," said Deirdre. "What I wonder is, are we lost?"

"Mom doesn't get lost," said Annabel. "It's her job. She knows where we are."

"But I don't know where we are," said Deirdre.

"You don't have to," said Till.

"Suppose I got separated from the group. Suppose I got lost from you guys. *I* should know where we are, in case that happens."

"It won't happen," said Till.

"Are there bears in the woods, Till?"

"I don't know. Probably not. Black bears, if

there are any, and they wouldn't hurt you."

"They shot the last timber wolf years and years ago. They have it stuffed, over at Ma 'Cille's Museum of Miscellanea," said Samuel.

"Wolf!"

"But wolves don't hurt you, anyway," Samuel went on. "We studied wolves. They're very organized and like a family. It's people that hurt wolves."

"Thank you, Farley Mowat," muttered Deirdre.

They straggled to a stop behind their mother. "What do you think of this one?" she asked.

Annabel walked around to the other side. "It's got a gap," she said. "Down low. Like it's lost a tooth."

"It looks a little tall to me," said Mr. Wyndham.

"It looks like the last tree we looked at," said Deirdre.

"Nooo . . ." Samuel bent forward, looking intently. "It's sort of crooked, too."

"Tough customers," said Mrs. Wyndham. "Come on, then." She wheeled and started back through the trees.

"Susannah — " Wyn Wyndham picked up his pace.

Till slowed down, struck by a sudden premonition. "This looks awfully familiar."

Annabel looked around. "Maybe we came here last year to cut down our tree."

"No. No. Annabel, see that gully over there? Didn't we go by it already?"

Annabel walked over to the gully and stared at it, as if by close inspection she might recognize it.

"How can you tell? Everything looks alike! I'm not going any further." Deirdre stopped dead.

"Look, Annabel. Remember that fallen sycamore? Right by the gully! And then this hill goes straight up behind it. We *have* gone by here . . . about 15 minutes ago. . . ."

"Are you listening to me? *Where* are we?" Deirdre's voice got even sharper.

Annabel turned and angled back onto the trail slightly ahead of them. "I think we're going in circles, Till," she said over her shoulder. "No, in *a* circle."

"We're lost!" Deirdre's voice went up. "I knew it! We're lost."

Samuel, who had been dawdling along behind, covertly inspecting Deirdre, suddenly let out a howl of outrage. "Mommmmm . . . !" He pushed past them and trotted ahead.

Annabel broke into a trot, too. "Where is he going? Where are you going, Samuel?"

Samuel didn't answer.

Till shook her head. "She got us." Picking up her pace, Till followed Annabel.

"You're doing this on purpose, aren't you? To scare me!"

"And we fell for it, too," said Till more to herself than anything.

"Stop right now!" shrieked Deirdre.

Till stopped, startled, and turned. Deirdre was standing as frozen as a deer in her tracks. She looked like a magazine advertisement: long slim perfect jeans tucked into boots, a slightly faded jeans jacket buttoned over a green L.L. Bean down vest. The red-and-green scarf was wound twice around her neck and looped so that one end hung down in front, one in the back. She had on green earmuffs. And her face was bright red with frustration and rage.

"You look like a Christmas tree," said Till, without thinking.

"What is that supposed to mean?"

"Nothing," said Till. "You're just all red and green."

"I suppose you think you're being funny?"

"Uh," said Till, "c'mon."

"Stop, stop, stop! I'm not going another step until you tell me *where we are*. Where are your father and mother? We're getting separated one by one, just like in those horror movies. Don't you dare leave me. I can't believe you're treating me like this. I don't have to take this!"

"Like what?" asked Till. "Mom's just playing a joke on us, that's all. Come on."

Deirdre put her hands on her hips, her face

still full of fury. "A joke? Are you making fun of me?"

"No! Mom's just got a weird sense of humor." Till held a branch aside and made a sweeping motion as if she were bowing. "Come *on*," she repeated.

Deirdre folded her arms and didn't move.

"Or we really will be lost," added Till.

Deirdre held her pose a moment longer, then brushed past Till with a swish that almost sizzled in the cold air.

Two minutes later they caught up with the others standing in a small clearing.

"Over here," said Till's mother, her voice full of laughter.

Till and Deirdre followed Annabel through a patch of underbrush and emerged suddenly in a small stand of pines, tall enough and old enough to have carpeted the ground beneath with needles. The needles gave up a sharp, soothingly familiar scent, a stronger distillation of the scent of the woods around them. The surrounding trees sheltered them all from the cut of the wind. The clearing was silent, scored across by the last shafts of the day's light.

To one side of the clearing was a tree neither short nor tall, round and straight, set slightly apart from all the other trees. For one moment they all stood, still as figures in a manger scene, around their Christmas tree.

7

All I Want for Christmas

"Do we have to cut it down? It's a beautiful tree, just where it is." Till broke the silence.

"It won't get a chance to grow much more here among these pines. It's probably already feeling the lack of light."

Till gave her mother a grateful look, forgetting all about Deirdre until she heard a tiny, delicate snort, dainty as a cat's, behind her.

"You tricked us," said Annabel to their mother.

"I wanted you to get good shopping value for your money. Suppose I'd led you right to this tree. You'd have been disappointed."

"When the going gets tough, the tough go shopping!" Deirdre stepped assuredly into the midst of the Wyndhams, and smiled sunnily at Mrs. Wyndham.

Mrs. Wyndham grinned back. "Exactly."

Till snorted, not a tiny, delicate snort, but, unfortunately, a sound more like a dog headfirst in a bowl of water. "*You* thought we were lost."

"We told you we weren't. Wolves. Bears!" Sam made his version of a wild animal sound.

"Come up to New York and we can play lost and found on the subways!" Deirdre rounded on Till and Sam, then drew herself up immediately. "I'm new to all this. I was a little disconcerted."

Disconcerted? thought Till. *Disconcerted?*

Deirdre swept on. "It's a fabulous tree. Fabulous."

It's like she never pitched a temper tantrum in the middle of the woods, thought Till in confused admiration.

Deirdre whirled and flashed her smile at Till, as if *she* had found the tree, just for Till. "Isn't it a fabulous tree, Till?"

"Fabulous," said Till weakly, her head spinning.

"We've never had such a beautiful tree," said Mr. Wyndham. "I'm not a man who likes to shop, Susannah, but this was worth it."

Their mother unhooked the ax and slid it out of the protective leather case. Till half turned her

59

head, knowing she would be glad to have the tree home, decorated, shining and bright, but not liking what it took to get it there.

Unexpectedly, Deirdre nudged Till. "What kind of tree is that?"

"Sycamore."

"And that?" Deirdre pointed at another tree, so that Till had to turn almost all the way around to see it. "A, a dogwood."

"And I know what these are." Deirdre knelt down. "Pinecones!" She held one aloft, twirling it. "You know, we could collect some and make a wreath, like you see in the magazines."

"We make special Christmas decorations every year," Till confessed, squatting down beside Deirdre. "But it's all homemade. I mean, I wanted to try some of the special stuff in a magazine I found, but Mom . . ." She shrugged.

"Mothers! Tell me about it!"

Deirdre began scooping up pinecones, inspecting each one. "C'mon, Till!" Together Deirdre and Till gathered pinecones, stuffing them in their pockets until the tree was down, the branches tied, and it was ready to go back home and be a Christmas tree.

"We've been here before!" cried Annabel joyously as they made their way back through the woods, and broke into laughter at her own joke.

And then their father began to sing. "We wish

you a Merry Christmas, we wish you a Merry Christmas."

Their mother took it up, and Annabel and Samuel began to shout out the words, exuberantly off-key.

Oh, no, thought Till. She was mortified. She glanced over at Deirdre. These are not my parents, she wanted to say. This is not my family. These are not my songs.

Then, with a shock, she realized that Deirdre was singing, too.

"This is so much fun." Deirdre laid a pinecone, which she'd just finished painting gold, on the newspaper spread out on the card table, and picked up another. "When we're done, we'll glue them all together, wreath-shaped, and tie a red bow on it and hang it on the front door."

"Look." Annabel held up a blown-out egg onto which she had meticulously crayoned an intricate series of green Christmas trees before dipping it into the red egg dye. "I'm going to decorate all the trees with sequins and glitter, so they'll be decorated like a real Christmas tree."

"Fabulous," said Deirdre.

Annabel beamed. Till bent back over her own egg, which she was decorating with a crazy quilt of colored sequins. Samuel, for reasons best known only to him, was dipping pieces of popcorn in the egg dye, and then gluing those to his egg.

"So, you do this every year," said Deirdre.

"Yep," said Samuel.

"You each make an egg every year?"

"Yep."

"You make one for Santa Claus, too?"

Samuel looked up. Annabel and Till did, too. "Nope," said Samuel. "But we leave him cookies."

"Have you ever *seen* Santa Claus?"

Till glanced quickly over at her mother and father, who were clipping lights onto the tree branches, moving in a sort of formal dance around each other.

"Nooo," Annabel said.

"Santa Claus is the spirit of Christmas," said Samuel firmly, and went back to his egg.

"I see." Deirdre finished up the last pinecone and reached for one of the blown-out hollow eggs. "Well. *I* am going to make an egg for St. Nick." Her eyes met Till's. "What's the matter, Till? If you get to leave the jolly old elf cookies, why can't I leave him an egg?"

"Fine," said Till shortly. Was Deirdre making fun of them?

As if she'd read Till's thoughts, Deirdre leaned over and whispered, "Yes, Till, there is a Santa Claus." She straightened up, picked up her egg, and began to paint with frowning concentration.

They worked in silence awhile. Then Deirdre said, "My egg is going to be the best. A fabulous Fabergé. By Deirdre."

Till didn't answer.

"The best," Deirdre repeated. "You know who Fabergé is, don't you? He was a world-famous jeweler. He made eggs of gold and silver and jewels for Russian royalty."

"I know," said Till.

"Do you?" Deirdre looked surprised, and not entirely pleased. "Well, he was the best. You should always be the best. That's my motto. Otherwise, what's the point?"

Till looked up. Deirdre was staring at her ferociously.

"Sure," said Till.

Deirdre stared at Till a moment longer, then turned her hand palm down and pressed her egg into red and green confetti on the table.

"Deirdre!" cried Till.

"Wow," said Annabel.

"Anything for Santa," said Deirdre calmly. "Besides, I can do better. Much better."

Till braced herself for whatever Deirdre might do or say next, but whatever it was got lost in a huge yawn.

"I'm simply ex-hausted," gasped Deirdre. "Sorry."

"You can go to bed," said Till quickly. "We leave

the table up until Christmas Eve, to keep making decorations, and wrap packages, and decorate those, and all that."

"Great." Deirdre pushed back from the table and stood up. "Good-night, Wyndhams," she said. "See you in the A.M." She waved as if she were exiting the stage in a play.

"Good-night," said Mrs. Wyndham, smiling. Till's father murmured something.

Till lifted her hand to wave, then lowered it, feeling foolish. "Night," she said softly. She looked down at her own egg, and her fingers tightened around it. Tacky, she thought. But she couldn't bring herself to break it.

Deirdre had been asleep when Till had gone up to bed not much later the night before. And she was asleep still the next morning, scrunched chin down on her pillow, as Till slid around her room, getting ready for school.

Somehow, she'd expected Deirdre to be a sort of Sleeping Beauty, lying face up, hands folded, prepared to wake up smiling and perfect just in case. But for all that her slippers were neatly side by side under the bed, and her quilted fuschia satin bathrobe, with its scrolled initial D, was folded precisely across the footboard of the bed, Deirdre slept scrunched down, in a warren of sheets and blankets.

Till heard the gurgle of coffee in the coffee

maker and knew her father was up, and breakfast was almost ready. She slipped quietly out of the room.

She was halfway through her bacon, grape jelly, and toast sandwich when Deirdre appeared at the door of the kitchen.

"Coffee!" gasped Deirdre.

Everyone except Mr. Wyndham looked up. Deirdre was standing in the door of the kitchen, her bathrobe trailing behind her.

"Aha!" Deirdre swooped down on the coffee pot. "Where're the cups?"

Till's father, hunched over his own coffee, muttered, "Cabinet." He took a tentative sip, as if trying to decide whether he was awake, or dreaming.

Deirdre filled her cup, adding milk, before she sat down. She took a swallow of coffee, then slammed down the mug and jumped up.

"Hot?" asked Till.

"I almost forgot. Wait right here."

"Where are we going to go?" asked Annabel, as Deirdre sailed out of the kitchen again.

"Literal-minded," said Till softly. "See?"

"She sure picks up steam fast, doesn't she?" their father interposed.

"Isn't that in the Beatitudes?" Till asked. "Samuel? Blessed are the early risers?"

Samuel said solemnly, unexpectedly, "The early bird getteth the worm."

"Hard on the early worms," said their father, and drooped back over his coffee.

Annabel turned her head back and forth, hanging onto the thread of the conversation for dear life.

"Here it is!" Deirdre danced back into the kitchen and thrust a shiny paper bag with a little bow looped around both handles toward their father. Still holding his coffee, Mr. Wyndham took the bag and set it down on the table.

"Thanks, Dei — "

"I'm sorry Mrs. Wyndham isn't awake yet."

"She's awake," said Samuel. "She's over at the mill."

"Oh. Well. Here. This is just a little something. I hope you like it."

Till finished her sandwich. Her father kept sitting there, looking vaguely confused, holding his coffee, not quite focusing on Deirdre's gift. Deirdre leaned over and pulled the bow loose.

"It's coffee," she explained. "Two kinds. Water-process decaffeinated, and chocolate-almond."

Till got up and put her plate in the sink. "I'm going to school now," she said. Her father made the sleepy sort of snorting noise that meant "Have a good day." Till waited to see if Deirdre would say, "Wait, I'll come with you." Or even, "School? Tell me all about it."

But Deirdre didn't.

"You want to walk with me, Annabel? Sam?"

"No," said Sam.

"Why?" said Annabel.

"Never mind," said Till, slinging her backpack over her shoulder.

"Good-bye!" she heard Deirdre call out cheerfully, just before the kitchen door slammed shut.

Till pressed against the bricks on the south side of the schoolhouse.

Despite the cold of the day, a thin layer of heat emanated from them. Like bricks made of red flannel, thought Till dreamily. She yawned with the cold. I'm surprised I haven't worn a hollow in these bricks, she thought. She could just see it, a neat little brass plaque someday: Till leaned here. . . .

The talk went on around her, where most of the sixth-graders were huddled for afternoon recess, sheltering from the wind. As usual, Sarie and Melanie and Lulinda stood nearby, but Till wasn't really part of the group. She wasn't part of any group at all, but today it felt fine to be invisible. Can people see right through me? she thought. To the bricks? Unless, when you're invisible, they see your clothes, but not you. But that would look pretty weird, a bunch of old clothes, propped up against the wall.

Lulinda's voice interrupted Till's ponderings.

"Huh?" said Till.

"Your friend from New York? Is she here?"

"Sure," said Till.

"Are we going to meet her, or what?" asked Sarie.

"Sure."

Melanie rolled her eyes.

"You will," said Till. "At the class Christmas party."

"I can hardly wait," said Lulinda.

Till ignored Lulinda after that. It was easy to do. Because for the rest of the day, Lulinda didn't even look her way.

8

O Little Town of Evergreen

They walked sedately through the town: Samuel, stiff in his Sunday best, in the lead, their parents in the middle with Peter, Deirdre and Till bringing up the rear, with Annabel wheeling impartially between them and whatever caught her attention along the way.

A crisp and shining universe wheeled above them, stars that shepherds might indeed watch by night, the air still and cold, catching sounds and making them resonate in the darkness. Each house seemed as jeweled as a vaudeville Fabergé egg, trees colorful in the windows, lights strung above lintels and around porches, wreaths on doors and candles in windows. In some places Santas and reindeers cavorted on lawns or rooftops.

"I love parties," said Deirdre. "Tell me about your aunt's party, Till. Tell me *everything*."

"Do you go to a lot of parties?" Till thought of the Christmas party coming up at school at the end of the week, two days before Christmas Eve.

"It depends on what you call parties. My mother takes me to openings. We went to the Guggenheim once. Not for an opening of her art. She was working there, then, as an art handler. She . . ."

Till took a deep breath. "Wait. Stop. What are you talking about?"

Deirdre stopped. She planted herself in the middle of the sidewalk and said slowly, loudly, "We went to the Guggenheim. We . . ."

"No! I understand what you're saying. I don't know what you mean." Till folded her arms, face to face with Deirdre, glad Deirdre couldn't really see her expression.

"What do you mean?"

"I don't know what a, an opening is. Just for starts."

"Oh . . . oh. Well, of course. An opening is like, you know, those opening nights for movies you see, only this is the opening night of an art exhibit. The first night it's put on display, you know."

"And your mother's an artist."

"Yes. Quite a good one. Only there's this awful prejudice against women artists. I mean, it's impossible."

"The Guggenheim?" Till prompted.

"A museum. It's round. Only that's not a good description. It was designed by Frank Lloyd Wright, and it's sort of a big hollow spiral on the inside, and you go up and up and up along the walls. . . . You'd like it, Till."

"And an art handler."

"Just what it is. You get paid to handle art, pack it, ship it. You have to do it just right, because it's *art*. If it gets damaged, you can't just, you know, go out and buy a new one."

"Okay," said Till. She hesitated. "I guess I sound pretty dumb."

"How would you know if you didn't ask?" Deirdre paused. "My mother's always saying that."

"What does your father do?" asked Till.

"Business. He's an actuary. Don't ask. Your father?"

"Dad? Business, too, I guess. He does the computer stuff at the Evergreen Logging Company."

Deirdre started walking again, catching Till's arm and spinning her around beside her as she walked by. "I have some questions for you, too, you know," she said. "But come on, we don't want to get left behind."

71

"I know the way," said Till.

"Junior timber cruiser." Deirdre grinned a shadowy grin.

"Trust me," said Till, grinning a shadowy grin of her own. "Go on. What else do you do in New York at Christmas? It must be wonderful."

"We always go to St. Patty's — St. Patrick's Cathedral — for Christmas Eve service," said Deirdre conversationally as they walked up the stairs to Aunt Clare's house. "Lots of people do; it's an event. It's in Manhattan. On Fifth Avenue," she added.

Fifth Avenue, thought Till reverently.

"Ma*til*da." In a swirl of flowing colored sleeves and clinking bracelets, Aunt Lenore gave Till a bear hug. "Don't say I've grown," said Till.

"Oh, you!" Aunt Lenore swatted Till lightly on the arm and turned to Deirdre. "And you're Till's friend, from up North. We're delighted to have you."

"Up North," Deirdre repeated and smiled, a warmed-over, secondhand sort of smile, in Till's opinion. "I'm delighted to be down South."

"Well, good." Aunt Lenore didn't seem to notice the nature of Deirdre's smile. "Now, go take the chill off, get yourselves some punch, and sprinkle cookies." She fluttered both hands at them and turned to the next guests.

"Sprinkle cookies?" asked Deirdre.

"C'mon." Till led Deirdre to the dining room

and shoved a cup of punch and a sugar cookie, sprinkled with red sugar, into her hands.

"Christmas punch, sprinkle cookies," said Till.

Deirdre took an experimental sip of punch, and a mouse's nibble of cookie. "They're sugar cookies."

"Uh-huh. The secret is in the food coloring. They're . . . they used to be my favorites. Aunt Lenore used to save the sugar and let me sprinkle them, and I used to call them sprinkle cookies. She's probably got some back there for Annabel to sprinkle now. I guess Peter'll be next. . . ."

Deirdre nodded absently, surveying the room. Till picked up a green sprinkle cookie and began to eat it, trying to imagine the room through Deirdre's eyes.

Beneath a miniature Christmas tree on a corner table, a heap of presents spilled onto the floor, at least one of which, Till knew, had her name on it. But her aunts wouldn't give it to her tonight. They'd bring it by on Christmas day.

A wood-and-plaster manger scene, old and chipped, stood on the mantel next to the Seth Thomas seven-day clock. Cedar branches lay along the back of the mantel, and at either end fat red candles burned down into their own centers, glowing red from within.

In the dining room, plain, sugared, and hot-spice pecans were heaped on silver dishes on the dining-room table near the punch. From the sideboard, steam rose from another bowl of cider, beneath which burned a small blue flame. An array of bottles stood on another tray nearby.

"Tillie!" One of the paper doll twins was leaning toward them, her perfect cutout smile in place, all the edges of her clothes as sharp as paper.

"Hey, Ms. Darning. Deirdre, this is Ms. Darning."

"How do you do?" said Deirdre, with distinct politeness.

"Hello, dear," said Ms. Darning. "Till, you tell that sister of yours, if I don't see her first, that I have magazines to cut up to make new clothes."

"Yes, ma'am," said Till.

"New clothes?" Deirdre asked as Ms. Darning threaded her way away from them.

"She and her sister, they're twins, they're retired, but they baby-sit — they used to baby-sit me. Whenever they did, they'd always bring this big box of paper dolls, really old ones, and magazines to cut up to make new clothes for them. They're . . ."

"Weird," said Deirdre. "Paper dolls." She was turning again, a slow twirl, studying the room.

"Who's that?" she hissed. "Talking to Sammy."

"Talking to Sammy? The minister, who else? I wonder if Sammy drives him crazy, too, with all his religious notions. You'd think . . ."

She stopped. Deirdre wasn't listening, just looking, looking, while all around everybody in their finery rustled and swished, and maybe twitched a little uncomfortably because such special clothes weren't worn often enough to have the easy fit of habit.

Till sniffed. The smells, sweet and sharp and penetrating, all mixed together, eddied around them: perfumes and aftershaves, and the smell of cold wool warming, and the smell of the fire in the living room. For a moment, Till imagined the smells were colors, swirling around them in currents as complex as the ocean. But, she thought, if the smells are colors, what are the sounds?

For the sounds were equally rich: voices sliding up and down the scale of greeting and gossip, love and malice, the ticking of the clock, steady as a heart, the firecracker pop of the burning logs in the fireplace, the clink of ice and silver and the jingle of bracelets and the to and fro of feet on the polished wood floors and the carpets like islands.

Sounds could have shape, maybe, thought Till. Shapes like . . .

"So these aren't all your relatives."

"I should hope not," said Till.

Deirdre looked past Till.

"Who's *that*? Talking to your mother?"

Till twisted to look. "Oh. Aunt Clare. My other aunt who's having the party."

"Go on," said Deirdre impatiently.

"Well . . . she's not my aunt, exactly. And she always wears one color, most of the time. Beige, like tonight. Or black. Or gray. Or if she wears more than one color, it's just one of those colors mixed in. She says it saves time, and then my aunt Lenore says . . ."

"*Really*. She doesn't look related at all. She's very elegant. She looks like, like, she looks like she could be going into St. Patty's . . . She's so . . ." Deirdre smoothed her skirt, gave her head a little toss.

Till frowned. Aunt Clare didn't look any different to her.

"Where's the bathroom?" said Deirdre.

"C'mon." Till showed Deirdre the way, then wound through everyone back out to the living room. Aunt Clare was still there, and Till studied her thoughtfully. Her aunt looked up and caught Till's eye and motioned her over.

"What do you think?"

"About the party?"

"The party first. Life in general second."

"It's a nice party," said Till. "When you were in New York . . ."

"Your father told me you might be interested."

"Uh-huh. When you were in New York, what was it like?"

"The streets are paved with gold, the women

76

are all bright and beautiful, the men are all handsome and rich. . . ."

"Aunt Clare!"

"It's a town," said her aunt. "It's a great town. It's a terrible town. It's a town like any other town. It's like no other place in the world."

"But what's it *really* like?" said Till.

"You'll find out," said her aunt.

"It'll take *forever*!"

"Don't count on it." Her aunt paused. "But after forever goes by, don't stop at New York. There's a whole world, and a whole lot of things to do."

"Then why are you here? Why didn't you stay?"

"Because," said her aunt, uncharacteristically looking away, around the room. She suddenly smiled and looked back at Till. "How about there's no place like home?"

"You can say that again," said Till darkly. Then she remembered something. "You're not from Evergreen anyway."

"How about . . . how about because someday, Till Wyndham, who you are is going to be more important than where you are, and what you think that makes you. And then, too, New York is always New York, and it is always there."

"I'm from New York." Deirdre had come back. She held out her hand. "Hello. I'm Deirdre. I'm visiting Till for Christmas." Deirdre smiled, really smiled this time.

Till saw little lights like the sparkle of Christmas ornaments dancing in her aunt's eyes. "But of *course*." Aunt Clare looked at Deirdre for just an instant, then said, "Do call me Clare. When you have a chance, I want to hear all about what's happening in New York. Such a fun little town."

Fun little town, thought Till.

"Of course, I'm sure it's changed. It's been too long. When I used to go there, before I lived there, I used to go up by train, one seat for me, one seat for my dancing dresses, so they wouldn't get wrinkled. Now I've got the wrinkles, so I just fly."

"Really?" said Deirdre. For once she seemed at a loss for words.

"Aunt Clare," said Till.

"The truth, Till, from me to you. Now, Deirdre, have you had any cake? Get Till to get you some."

"Hey," said Till. "No fair." But she was grinning.

"Merry Christmas!" Aunt Clare lifted her eyebrows Groucho Marx style and was gone.

Till stared after her.

So did Deirdre. "I like your aunt," she said.

"So do I," said Till, surprising herself.

"So, what're you, her favorite?"

"Me? No." Till was even more surprised by that. "What do you mean?"

"I don't know. Just the way she talked to you, I guess."

"She does give me a lot of grief," said Till slowly. "Not like anyone else. Just me."

"See," said Deirdre.

"Mmm," said Till. She thought about what her aunt had said, and what Deirdre had said, too.

But Deirdre was already spinning off, following her own thoughts in another direction.

"Hey, Till. Who's that? Who's Samuel talking to now? Does he only talk to grown-ups?"

Reluctantly, Till focused on what Deirdre was saying. But all the rest of the night she couldn't help thinking that maybe Aunt Clare didn't just like her, Till, because she was family. Maybe Aunt Clare liked Till for herself, too.

And she was thinking of all the questions she was going to ask her, as soon as she had a chance.

9

What Child Is This?

"**W**hat? You told the Flame of Life Baptist Church what? When?"

"At the party," repeated Samuel patiently.

Mrs. Wyndham closed her eyes, then opened them again, as if she were hoping that somehow Samuel had disappeared from her sight.

"Neat," said Annabel, bounding up the front steps of the house and pushing the door open.

"Don't run," said Mrs. Wyndham automatically. "It's out of the question, Sam. I want you to call whoever it is you talked to — "

"Mrs. Gladiolus," supplied Sam.

"Phyllis Gladiolus. Great. Of all the people in all of the churches, you had to walk into hers. . . ."

"I didn't go to her church. I asked her at the Christmas party. Right before we left."

Till's mother turned and looked back down the street, as if she could see Mrs. Gladiolus still at Aunt Clare's party. "Thank you, Clare," she muttered.

"The Southern Baptists are real primitive, right?" asked Deirdre suddenly. "Against the ERA and all that."

"Not just the Southern Baptists, and not just the Baptists," said Till's mother, with careful patience. "But, yes, Phyllis Gladiolus thinks a woman's place is limited to Kinder, Kirche, and Kuche."

They were in the front hall now, shedding outer layers of clothing. And emerging, thought Till, just like butterflies, colorful in their Christmas clothing.

"What's that?" asked Annabel.

"Aren't you Baptists?" asked Deirdre.

"No. Samuel . . ."

Annabel tried again. "What's . . . ?"

"Children, church, and kitchen, Annabel. Samuel . . ."

"I think it's a good idea, Mom," said Samuel indignantly. "Peter'd make a perfect Jesus."

They all looked over at Peter, who was concentrating intensely on a piece of banana he was carrying in one fist.

"Hey, listen, Susannah, maybe it's not such a bad idea." Mr. Wyndham said slowly.

"I do not want to in *any way* support a church that believes I don't have equal rights in the eyes of God, not to mention my fellow citizens!"

"Well, for Pete's sake, neither do I. . . ."

"For Pete's sake. You made a joke, Dad. Get it? For Pete's sake!"

"Quit trying to change the subject, young man."

Till concentrated on hanging up her coat as intently as Peter was studying the mashed banana. How humiliating. Life wasn't hard enough, that now Samuel had to go and make it even worse. And just as things were getting better, she concluded not very clearly.

"Mom," said Samuel.

"You think you get brownie points with God because of this?" Till suddenly burst out. "You think God leans over and says, 'Hey, let's put another rung on old Samuel Wyndham's ladder to heaven, for signing up his baby brother to be in the Living Manger, right there in Evergreen, Alabama'? Huh?"

"Till!" Mrs. Wyndham.

"It's all right. I forgive her." Sammy snarled a smile at Till.

"How dare you forgive me! *I* don't want to be forgiven!"

Beside her, Deirdre suddenly began to laugh. "Way to go, Till."

"Deirdre . . ." began their mother, looking shocked.

"Don't you dare laugh at me." Till turned her fury on Deirdre, but Deirdre wasn't fazed.

"I'm not laughing at you. Just admiring your style."

That stopped Till. "Huh?"

"Your way with words . . . but, listen, I think it's a good idea."

"You could just let it be for one night," said Annabel, extracting a handful of sprinkle cookies, all broken into bits and pieces, from her coat pocket. "And then it would be sort of a Christmas gift."

Susannah Wyndham slammed the door of the hall closet shut and everyone jumped.

"Now, listen, every one of you, and listen close. Peter may be a Baptist Jesus stand-in for *one* night, *if* that night isn't too cold, and *if* it isn't raining. In exchange, you, Samuel, are going to learn a little basic sewing. We'll start with putting buttons back on shirts."

"No way!"

"Honor your father and mother, or your days are numbered. . . ." hissed Till, but now she had her eye on Deirdre, who started laughing again.

"Yes, you will. Till and Annabel know how. Your father knows how. It's time you learned. And don't you dare say it's girls' work. In fact, now that I think of it," she rounded on Mr. Wyndham, "your father is the one who's going to teach you. And when Peter gets old enough, you are going to teach him. We're starting some new traditions. Right now."

Samuel opened his mouth again, then closed it.

"Away in a manger," said Deirdre.

"And away we go," said Mr. Wyndham. "Hot chocolate, anyone?"

"Your brother Sam is too much," said Deirdre, falling back on her bed. "Which one was Mrs. Gladiolus?"

"I don't remember seeing her. She's tall. Like an Amazon."

"But is she single-breasted like one?" asked Deirdre.

"Yes," said Till.

Deirdre rolled over and looked seriously into Till's eyes. "Are you telling the truth? How do you know?"

Till stared back and said solemnly, "She's mono-breasted. She has one big bosom, and it goes straight across." Till made a gesture. "Like this!"

Deirdre gave a shriek of laughter. "Mono-breasted! The latest in Amazon fashion! Till, you're too much! Your whole family is too much. . . ."

Till was laughing, too.

"Girls. It's late." Her father's voice came faintly to them down the hall from the kitchen.

"Listen, Deirdre, I have an idea. Want to sleep in the living room?"

"Why?"

"You know, like a spend-the-night party. We can get the sleeping bags out of the utility room and sleep in front of the fireplace, with the Christmas tree lights on. It's really fun."

"Tonight?" said Deirdre doubtfully.

"Well . . . not tonight, maybe. I did that one Christmas Eve when I was little. I told Mom and Dad I was going to catch Santa."

"Cute."

"Yeah. Anyway, I went to sleep in front of the fire and when I woke up, I was in my own bed. And the stockings were all filled, and there were all these presents under the tree, and the Coke we'd left for him had been drunk."

Deirdre gave a spurt of laughter, smothering it in her pillow. "Coke! We leave Dr. Brown's Cream Soda."

"No wonder Santa's so fat!" Till hissed, and they both started laughing again, more now that they were trying to be quiet.

Then Deirdre said, "Hey, I have an idea. Let's do it *this* Christmas Eve."

Now it was Till's turn to be doubtful. "I don't know. I don't think they'd let us do it on Christmas Eve *now*."

"We won't tell them. We'll sneak down after everybody's asleep. And if Santa's already come — you know? — it'll be cool and we'll tell Annabel and Samuel and everyone we slept right through it."

"What if we're there first?"

"Well, then, maybe we'll wake up in our own beds. What do you think, Till? Are you in?"

"Well . . ."

"C'mon. Please?"

"Well . . ." Till had an inspiration. "If you'll come to my class Christmas party."

"At school? When?"

"Friday. It's not even a whole school day. Everyone . . . uh, some of my, my friends know you were coming to visit. From New York and all."

"Okay. Okay. Agreed." Deirdre leaned over from her bed and held out her hand, palm out. "Mono-minded!"

Till leaned over and slapped Deirdre's hand, and grinned. "Mono-maniacs!" she said.

10

Silver Bells

The last day of school before Christmas, the morning of the Christmas party, the world was made of silver glass. Till woke to an uncanny silence, and a room full of pale, glinting light, as if the full moon were pressed directly against her window. She raised her head and squinted, and saw that the pale light was gold *and* silver: The sun was shining through the window, but a window glazed with ice.

Till looked over at Deirdre. But she was still asleep.

As quietly as possible, Till slid out of her own

bed and tiptoed over to the window. She blew on the pane of glass until her breath warmed a circle of ice to water, and cleared a place where she could see out. Peering through, she saw that it must have rained sometime the night before, and that the rain had frozen as it fell. The branches of the trees were coated with ice, and knobby frozen drops hung beneath every branch. The stir of the wind made the glittering branches rub together with a musical tinkling sound, thousands and thousands of faint, icy windchimes.

For one second Till felt happy, a happiness like Christmas and birthdays and last days of school, or doing something right and knowing it. For one second she was absolutely motionless, staring out at the still, shining world, and wishing it would never go away.

"Stay," she breathed, but even as she wished, the wishing made the silver world slide out of reach into memory.

Then she sensed she was being watched. She turned and saw that Deirdre was awake.

"Come look," she said softly, and leaned to one side as Deirdre got out of bed, slid her feet into her slippers, and came to kneel beside Till.

"Wow," said Deirdre. "What happened?"

"It rained and then it froze," said Till.

"I've never seen that happen. . . . It's as beautiful as a first snowfall."

"I've never seen much snow before," said Till.

Deirdre looked over her shoulder at Till. "Will there be school today?"

Till shrugged. "The one time I remember it snowing, and sticking, everything closed down."

"I hope it doesn't today," said Deirdre. "We've got a party to go to!"

The ice storm didn't close things down. The ice was melting even as they spoke, and when they got down to breakfast, the radio on the kitchen counter was crackling with news: Parts of the state were closed. Birmingham was being shut down. Businesses and roads were being closed, announcement by announcement. But when the local news came on, Evergreen was still open. It hadn't been hit as hard as the rest of the northeast part of the state.

"Come on, then," said Deirdre, finishing the last of her coffee.

"Yeah," said Till.

Ms. Jungwirth introduced Deirdre to the class. Till, watching Lulinda out of the corner of her eye, borrowed words from her Aunt Clare: Lordy but I'm in my glory. For not anything that Lulinda could say or do would change the fact that Deirdre was there, and that she said, smiling slightly, not too friendly, not easily, but just right, "Thank you. I'm glad Till invited me."

And even better, when everyone turned to look

at Till, who knew this sleek and shining girl, who was really and truly friends with her, Till, even in her glory, was smart enough at last not to beam or squirm or look modest. She looked straight back at Lulinda, and raised her eyebrows just a little, and it was Lulinda who looked away.

Then when they finished playing the silly Christmas games, like pin-the-tail-on-the-reindeer, and applauded as Ms. Jungwirth unwrapped her gift from the class, a complete, new dictionary — "*Un*-bowdlerized," she exclaimed happily, flipping through the pages — and were standing around, waiting to be dismissed, Lulinda said, "Of course, there's not much to do around here."

Deirdre laughed. "Well, maybe not for you, but Till is, like, a party animal, you know? We're going out again tonight. And we have a surprise party planned for Christmas Eve." Deirdre looked at Till and winked slightly.

"Oh," said Till, and winked slightly back. "I'm glad you reminded me!"

Then Melanie said, "*Are* you getting your ears pierced, Till?" She'd turned to Deirdre. "I am. For Christmas."

Deirdre said, "Oh."

A small silence fell. "I guess I'm not," said Till at last. "Not until I'm older. Sixteen, or maybe a hundred."

Lulinda laughed, then, and so did Sarie, and

Till did, too. But Melanie, never one to let well enough alone, said, "Poor Till," in a tone that didn't mean poor Till at all.

"Well," said Deirdre. "Everyone in New York has pierced ears." And her tone said, big deal.

And then the bell rang, and Till and Deirdre said, almost at once, "Well, Merry Christmas, " and then started laughing. They left together, walking part of the way with Lulinda and Sarie and Melanie.

Bliss. I will never forget this day as long as I live, thought Till, waving as she and Deirdre left the others and rounded the corner and headed down the street.

And then it happened. Somehow, Deirdre slipped, on some last bit of the silver ice maybe, caught in a corner of cold shade. She slipped, and threw out her arms, and staggered backwards, flailing, and then forwards, and then, as Till stood there, frozen, Deirdre crashed down on the sidewalk, her sharp-heeled shoes going right out from under her.

Till, after a gasp, started to laugh.

Deirdre sat, stunned. Till stuttered out, trying to stop laughing, "Oh! Is that ice-skating New York style?"

She went toward Deirdre, reaching out her hand. Then she stopped.

Deirdre was looking up at Till, her eyes squeezed almost shut, her face pale and pinched.

She said, in a voice as cold and full of hate as anything Till had ever heard, "Get away from me!"

"What? Are-are you all right?"

"Get . . . away . . . from . . . me. Now!" Deirdre struggled to her feet, shifted gingerly, then straightened up. Her eyes narrowed again, and the paleness of her face became suffused with red.

"How dare you?" she hissed.

Till took an involuntary step back. "What?"

"How dare you laugh at me! I could have been killed! Or crippled."

"I'm sorry, I . . ."

"After all I've put up with! You think I wanted to be here? You think I asked to come to this hick town to spend a hick Christmas when I could have been . . . after all I've done for you! Letting myself be put on exhibit, practically, for your stupid, mean, tacky — isn't that your word? TACKY friends."

"But."

"Till Wyndham, you can go to . . . but wait. You already live in Evergreen, Alabama. Don't you?"

Before Till could say another word, Deirdre stalked away, neither running nor looking down at the sidewalk that had tripped her up, leaving Till alone in the glare of the cold December afternoon sun.

11

The Season to Be Jolly

"Till."

A mosquito, thought Till, does that. Hovers just out of reach.

"Till?"

Annabel was hovering on the threshold of Till's room. Again. Just at the edge of her vision . . .

"Till — "

. . . getting on her *nerves*. "What?"

"Are you mad at me, Till?"

"What? Why?"

"Cause you sound like you are."

It would be nice, thought Till, to have eyes in

the back of my head. I'd just reach back, part my hair, and glare.

"Are you?"

"No, I'm not mad at you. Go away. Okay?"

"You promise?"

"I promise."

"Good."

Till waited. Then she said, "You're not going away, are you?"

"I have to tell you something."

Swinging around so quickly that she caused Annabel to jump back, Till scanned her room quickly, trying to tell if anything was missing or broken. "Tell me what?"

"In the living room," said Annabel, retreating. Till had no choice but to follow.

Annabel stopped at the card table, heaped more lavishly than ever with the debris of wrapping gifts and making decorations. She picked something up and turned slowly.

"Okay, okay," said Till. "What is it?"

"I broke it." Annabel held out her hand. Till's Christmas egg, row upon row of overlapping sequins, was crumpled along one side, held together by a mangy scattering of sequins and glue.

"I didn't mean to. It was dry, and I just picked it up, and then it slipped, and then I grabbed it. . . ."

Till kept staring at her egg.

"Till?"

94

"I'm busy. I'm busy being *speechless*."

"Till!" wailed Annabel.

Till reached out and took the egg from Annabel and held it up. "Stop. Please. How can I be speechless if you're making all that noise? Look, it's not exactly broken."

Annabel got calmer. She gave a little experimental sniff.

"It's more, more crackled. Maybe we can fix it." Motioning to Annabel to join her, Till sat down at the table. "Maybe we can suction out the dented part with a piece of tape." Till carefully laid a piece of tape over the damaged part of the egg and tried peeling it gently off. Some of the egg pulled back into egg shape. But a piece of the shell peeled off along with the tape. Now the shell had a hole in it.

Annabel sniffed again.

"I wonder what Santa Claus would say about this," Till said thoughtfully.

Her little sister's face turned bright red. Her mouth dropped open.

"I'm kidding. I'm kidding, okay? You are so — " Till stopped herself just in time. "Listen. Listen, I'll make a new one."

"There's not time," said Annabel.

"No? No, I guess not. Well, then we'll hang it up anyway. We'll just put the crumbled part facing away from everyone. So only the tree can see it, right?"

Annabel bent her head. "I'm sorry."

Holding the egg up to her sister's ear, Till said, "Listen, Annabel. Wouldn't it be great if you could hold an egg up to your ear and hear the ocean, the way you can with a shell? Or maybe Christmas sounds — you know, elves singing at the North Pole?"

Annabel listened a moment, then gave her sister a tentative smile, and shook her head. "I don't hear any elves."

"No? No elves? No ocean, either? Well, what if you could look inside and see a little town, like under a microscope, except with people instead of amoebas?"

Annabel put her hand over Till's and drew the egg close to her eye, peering through the hole. "I think I see something," she said. ". . . maybe."

"Maybe?"

"Maybe . . ."

"Well, that settles it, then. This egg is definitely better off the way it is, with a window in it. Let's put it on the tree, okay?"

Till picked up the egg, went over to the tree, and hung it up by the loop of ribbon glued to the top of the shell.

"There," said Till.

"There," said Annabel.

She and Till smiled at each other.

Annabel looked past Till, and smiled wider. "Hi, Deirdre."

Till went from feeling good and kind and wise to stammering anger all in a moment. She turned around. "You! How long have you been there?"

Deirdre jerked back, as if Till's anger was the last thing she expected. Before she could answer, Till stormed on. "Oh, excuse me. I forgot. You're so much better than all of us! The . . . the ice princess of the Evergreen sidewalks!"

Deirdre's face turned as red as Annabel's had a few minutes before, but she didn't say anything. As Till glared at her, she wheeled away. Till turned, too, and then the two of them, as if they were about to fight a duel, marched in opposite directions, Till out the door to the dining room, Deirdre back down the hall.

"Hey!" said Annabel.

The sound of two doors being slammed, at opposite sides of the house, as sharp as the sound of duelling pistols perhaps, was the only answer she got.

That night when she came back from taking her bath, Till was relieved to see that Deirdre was already in bed. Pretending that she believed Deirdre really was asleep, Till slid quietly between the covers of her own bed.

But she couldn't go to sleep. She felt bad, fighting with someone who was sharing her room. But she felt angry, too, more and more angry as she thought about what Deirdre had said.

Then Till thought, well, I feel the same way about Evergreen and all. I *do*.

Still, she argued with herself, it's not the same. Deirdre's company. Is that any way for company to act?

But is that any way for me to treat a guest?

I didn't. I didn't treat her any way at all. She started it.

Wonder what Santa Claus would think, thought Till, remembering her words to Annabel. She sighed and rolled over to face in the direction of Deirdre's bed.

Christmas. Day after tomorrow, and Deirdre's parents coming tomorrow afternoon.

She closed her eyes and tried to imagine herself in Christmases to come, real Christmases the way she wanted them to be.

But she couldn't. Christmas, whatever she might want it to be, was home, her family, even all the maddening things they did and said. That was Christmas, too.

What a day it had been. Deirdre had been perfect, just perfect. It had been better than show-and-tell in first grade, when she'd . . .

Till's thoughts slammed up against themselves. Show-and-tell. She opened her eyes.

As if Deirdre were something you take to class and show around for points . . . that's what I've been doing. That's how I've been treating her.

Tiptoeing around her, trying to make her be a certain way. And she's not. She's smart, and she looks good, and she's from New York. But she's also quick-tempered, and paranoid, and . . . and nice. Look what she's put up with. And she's a long way from her family and her home, for Christmas, too.

Till turned to look at Deirdre's dim shape.

"Deirdre," she whispered, softly. She listened. The sound of Deirdre's breathing was steady, even, the firmly-committed-to-sleep sound of someone really asleep.

Till rolled back over. How could Deirdre sleep at a time like this?

And then, just as she was starting to get annoyed all over again, she fell asleep herself.

The Saturday sound of the vacuum cleaner woke Till on Christmas Eve morning. That in itself was not unusual since it was a Saturday as well as Christmas Eve. But Till's father had vacuumed the house once already that week, and the smell of baking was definitely not a Saturday one, nor a Christmas one, at least not so early in the morning.

"Deirdre?" muttered Till, remembering what she'd been thinking about the night before. But Deirdre was up and gone. Till saw by the clock that it was just as early in the morning as she'd thought, but Deirdre's bed was already a folded envelope, her bedroom slippers aligned at the side.

"Good morning," Till said to the empty bed. "Merry Christmas." She rolled back over and buried her head beneath her pillow in a cowardly way and made herself go back to sleep.

Vacuuming had given way to polishing when Till finally came down the stairs. Annabel was dusting and polishing tables and chairarms and whatever struck her fancy; Samuel, mutinously, was polishing the good silverware; Deirdre, sitting at the dining room table beside him, was wiping off glasses and plates from the china cabinet behind her. In the front hall, Till found her father polishing the little panes of glass at the top of the front door.

Till wandered toward the kitchen and found her mother wiping the counter in an abstracted sort of way.

"Hey."

"Ummm," said her mother.

"I'm hungry."

"Cereal."

"Cereal?" What kind of breakfast was that on a Christmas Eve?

Her mother bent to peer in the oven without answering.

"Great," said Till. She made herself a bowl of

cereal and heaped the sugar on it. That would show her mother.

Her mother straightened up, catching Till in mid-heap. "Oh, good."

"Huh?"

"Sheets."

Till poured the sugar on her cereal, ate a syrupy bite, and waited.

"Now that you're here," said her mother, "you can put the sheets on the sofa bed in the den."

"Do you mind if I finish breakfast first?" asked Till.

It was wasted on her mother. "Of course not, dear." Her mother bent to study the oven again.

By noon, Till's patience was wearing thin. "It's supposed to be Christmas, not Spring Cleaning," she muttered, sweeping the front porch, even though the wind was as cold as a wet winding sheet and no one was going to linger long enough to notice if the stairs were swept or not.

She went back just in time to find Deirdre in the kitchen, talking to her mother. Till stopped in the doorway.

"Out of things like holly, and dried leaves. Some of the leaves are still quite beautiful. I could go get some now."

"What a good idea," Till's mother said. "There's a tall vase in that cabinet over there. You'll need the footstool."

She caught sight of Till. "Till, reach Deirdre down that tall vase out of the top cabinet."

"Aren't you going to the airport?" Till blurted out.

Deirdre raised her eyebrows. "No," she said coolly.

Silently, torn between her old anger and her new way of seeing Deirdre, or trying to see her, Till got the vase while Deirdre pulled on her jacket.

"Why don't you go with Deirdre, too, Till?"

"No, thank you," said Till, not at all coolly.

Her mother paused but before she could say anything, Samuel burst into the kitchen.

"Mom! Can I give Peter his bath? It's almost time."

"Time?" Mrs. Wyndham half-raised her wrist to look at her watch, which she wasn't wearing, almost dumping a tray of cheese straws, then caught herself at the last minute, and looked at the clock on the stove.

"Time. Thank you, Samuel."

In a flurry of movement, she straightened up, set the cheese straws on the rack on the counter to cool, slid the tin they were to go into out next to them, stripped off her apron and hung it behind the door, and began to rap out orders like a drill sergeant:

"Till, put the straws in here when they're cool. Samuel, give the kitchen floor one more sweep after Till does that. Are there guest towels in the downstairs bathroom?"

"Mom," said Till. "I did that already."

"Extra towels in the den?"

"Mom . . ."

Deirdre moved calmly out the back door.

Mrs. Wyndham bustled out the kitchen door, still talking. "Where's Annabel? Wyn? Wyn, it's almost time to leave for the airport."

Till went over to the counter, dumped the hot cheese straws into the container, and went into the den to watch the dumb Christmas parades that had already started on TV.

"They're heeere."

"Good old Annabel Revere," muttered Till, who'd spent an hour and a half on the sofa in the den, after her parents had left to drive to the airport. She'd gone to her room to get ready, and Deirdre had caught her with one foot in and one foot out of her pants, hopping around.

"Do you mind?" Till had snarled.

"Not at all," Deirdre had answered. "Just call me when you're finished."

Till had taken her own sweet time after that, although she could not say the results were impressive, even though she had ironed her shirt. Then she'd gone back down to the den to wait, without calling Deirdre.

She came out into the front hall to find Deirdre

standing in the door to the living room, blank-faced and frozen.

"They're heeere," mimicked Till softly. "Should we line up and curtsy?"

Deirdre jerked her chin sharply around. But she only said, "Suit yourself." She remained where she was as Annabel came thundering up to throw open the front door.

"Where's Sam?" asked Till.

"Giving Peter a bath," said Annabel.

"Still?" Before Till could pursue the question, the front door opened and then the front hall filled up with a blast of cold air and people.

One of the people, short, short as Till, with hair the color of ripe plums, and a coat made of patches like a quilt, detached herself from the group.

"Deedsy," she cried. "Baby." And flung herself on Deirdre.

Deirdre held her ground, raised her arms, and made a vague patting gesture against the back of the coat. Then she stepped back. "Hello, mother," she said.

"Loaves and fishes!" breathed Till, completely astounded. A tall, somber-looking man emerged from the background as Deirdre pulled back from her mother, and held out his hand solemnly. "Deirdre."

"Father," said Deirdre equally solemnly, taking his hand. She leaned forward, stood on her toes as he stooped, and kissed his cheek. Then she stepped back and released his hand.

"I *can't* believe we're here. After all these years. And I can't believe I said that. Don't I sound just like our *mothers,* Susannah? And this must be Matilda."

"It's Till." Till stepped back hastily and stuck out her hand. Deirdre's mother gave it a little tug, as if to pull Till into her embrace. Till planted her feet firmly, determined not to yield. For one awful moment, she thought they were going to get into a tug of war. Then Mrs. Frances swung around.

"And you're — "

"Annabel."

"Darling!" Annabel, who did not have Till's foresight, got scooped up and held, her feet dangling slightly above the floor.

"Put me down," said Annabel, in a muffled sort of way. "Please."

"Adorable. But Susannah, aren't there more?"

As if on cue, Samuel charged into the hall. Under one arm he held Peter, dry except for his slightly damp hair, and naked entirely. In the other hand he brandished a blanket. "Hey," he cried.

"Samuel! Peter!" said Till's mother.

"Uh-oh," said Annabel.

"How do you do," said Deirdre's father, as solemnly as ever, but Till caught a faint ripple of laughter beneath his words. Till's father stepped into the breach.

"Here's the rest of the family — Samuel, and there under his left arm, his brother Peter."

Deirdre's mother started to laugh.

"Say hello, Samuel," prompted Till, sweetly.

"Hello," said Samuel. "Mo-om. Listen! How do you do it? Peter keeps wiggling out. How do you wrap a baby in swaddling clothes?"

12

Away in a Manger

Still laughing, Deirdre's mother reached for Peter. "Swaddling clothes! That's right. Standing in for the Baby Jesus, one night only, Peter Wyndham. How *do* you swaddle a baby, Susannah?"

Now Till's mother was laughing, too. "I don't know. Till, Deirdre, Annabel, take their stuff into the den, and we'll take this unswaddled heathen into the living room and find out."

"I'll get the suitcases," said Mr. Frances.

"Let me help, Theo," said Till's father. "I'll show you the way to the den. You kids run on and swaddle Peter. . . ."

Annabel shot into the living room after the others and as quickly as it had filled up, the front hall emptied out, leaving Deirdre and Till standing there, in the backwash of voices.

"No, I can't let you — " Till's mother said.

"Listen, trust me, Susannah, if you were Mary, wouldn't you swaddle your baby in something nice and bright and colorful?"

"But not your coat — "

Samuel came back out. "Peter has to wear real clothes underneath. You think his pajamas are okay?"

"If they're warm enough," said Till absently. "Or that one-piece jumpsuit of his — that's warm."

Samuel nodded. "Yeah." He disappeared down the hall.

Till turned to say something to Deirdre, but she had slipped out. From the living room, she heard Deirdre's voice.

"Mother. Not your coat."

"I have a red blanket on my bed," said Annabel.

"Fabulous," said Deirdre quickly. "And listen, I have this wonderful scarf that Mrs. Wyndham made. Mother, you remember?"

"What a great idea." Till's mother sounded relieved.

"I'll get my blanket. You want your scarf, Deirdre?"

"Out in the hall on the stand," said Deirdre. "Thanks."

Annabel came out as Samuel passed Till, holding the jumpsuit.

"I've got it." Till took the scarf off the coatrack. "Go get the blanket."

Till went into the living room, where Samuel had taken on the chore of jostling Peter into his outfit.

"Here," she said.

Deirdre's mother looked up and seized both of Till's hands again in a bone-cracking squeeze. "A mind reader!" she cried.

"I was in the hall . . ." Till began but got no further. Mrs. Frances had gone on, talking about the various ways of folding scarves and how blankets might be folded the same way to swaddle a baby. Till's mother had started laughing again.

We might as well be invisible, thought Till, watching her mother and Mrs. Frances carry on. Briefly, her eyes met Deirdre's, and she wondered what Deirdre was thinking. But she couldn't tell.

An angel came out of the front door of the Flame of Life Baptist church and flew toward their car as they pulled to a stop in the circular driveway.

"You can't park here," said the angel, panting a little and turning into a tan brown girl not much older than Till. A silver halo on a headband bobbled above her head.

"The Baby Jesus can park anywhere he wants," said Till softly.

"Till," hissed Samuel, who was holding Peter, appropriately swaddled from head to toe.

"We're delivering the baby for the living manger," said Mr. Wyndham. "Samuel?"

Samuel hoisted Peter onto his shoulder and slid out of the car.

"Oh! Well — come on, then. It's almost time. Hurry up."

"If she were really an angel, she'd be a timekeeper angel, in heaven," remarked Mr. Frances.

"Or a traffic cop," said Deirdre unexpectedly.

The angel turned. "Parking is over to one side. I've got to get someone to come put the chain up across the driveway."

"See?" said Deirdre, and if Till hadn't known better, she would have thought Deirdre was talking to her.

The Living Manger was only for an hour since it was Christmas Eve. The families of the Living Manger actors had gathered inside in the church hall, where they stood, talking and drinking hot cider and hot chocolate, and taking turns going out into the cold to view the manger scene.

The Wyndhams and the Franceses joined the others, standing in one corner of the hall. Near the door, a snake jungle of cords and wires ran out to the manger scene, including a wire to the electric blanket that was one of the swaddling clothes wrapping Peter.

"They could power the Grateful Dead," said Till's father, studying the apparatus thoughtfully. Annabel's head swung in the direction of the graveyard next to the church.

"Not those dead people, Annabel," said Till quickly. "He means a, a rock group. Right, Dad?"

"From the *old* days," said Till's father. "Although they've endured . . ." He smiled suddenly. "Your mom and I once spent the night on the student union lawn in college so we would have a good spot for their concert the next day."

To Till's complete mortification, her mother suddenly launched into an air guitar gyration.

"Wait," said her father. "First, you have to tune up."

"Jeans!" cried Deirdre's mother. "Imagine jeans while you're at it."

"And long hair! And a tie-dyed T-shirt!"

Now they were all starting to strum the air and rock. "Dah, dah, dahdahdah da-ah," crooned Till's father.

People in the church hall began to turn and stare.

"Thank you, Jesus," muttered Till and fled into the cold.

* * *

111

Although it was Christmas Eve, and growing late, the press of people hadn't lessened. A steady stream was turning into the parking lot, on the other side of the church, and making its way to the front of the manger scene.

Till slipped into place at one end of the rope that held the crowd back, and lifted her burning cheeks to the cool night air. Her parents. If it wasn't one thing, it was another. When I grow up, she thought.

Someone edged into place beside her, and Till realized it was Deirdre. The loop of carols coming over the loudspeaker paused for a moment, and Till whispered, hesitantly, "Are they still doing it?"

"No."

"Good."

"They're singing old Beatles songs."

"Great! Just great."

"Hark the herald . . ." the carol began, and Till turned her attention back to the manger scene. Bathed in the spotlights, it looked as if it were set on the moon. In one corner, a donkey, a cow, and a sheep stood tethered. The donkey was just standing there, the cow was chewing, and the sheep had folded its legs under itself and then lay down to sleep. Kneeling on the flat roof above the shed, next to the loudspeaker, was the traffic cop angel, her arms outstretched. Mary and Joseph sat, one on each side of the crib, where Peter lay angelically still. Just outside the manger, near the sheep, stood two shepherds holding shepherd's crooks, and on the other side, three wise men, holding boxes.

Till's mind went critically over the scene. It was made of false beards, and robes fashioned from bedsheets, and jewelry boxes for the frankincense and myrrh. The music came from a speaker, not a heavenly host, and the star was a spotlight, framed in silver foil spikes. The only real things were the animals and the straw. Tacky, said Till to herself.

Beside her, Deirdre was equally intent on the scene.

"Tacky," said Till aloud, softly. "Isn't it?"

The ragged wind picked up. The angel's silver cardboard wings flapped, the bedsheets on the shepherds and kings fluttered, the music was snatched away.

"No. I don't know. I've never seen anything like it."

"I bet," said Till. Then she leaned forward, studying one of the shepherds. "I don't believe it," she breathed. "Look!"

Her sudden movement had caught the attention of the shepherd, too. He shifted with equal suddenness, so only the edge of his face showed.

But it was too late. "Melanie," hissed Till. "That's Melanie!"

"Where?"

"The shepherd. In the plaid bathrobe . . ."

Till and Deirdre stared fixedly at the shepherd. It was too much. The shepherd broke, and looked back at them, and even in the pale lunar glow of the spotlights, Till could see the creep of color from beneath the shepherd's beard.

"I don't believe this. Wait'll I tell Sarie and Lulinda," said Till.

The music finished its loop again. The crowd shifted and waited, but the music was finished. The Living Manger was over.

Slowly, slowly, people began to shift, murmuring softly. Till looked up and realized that her family and Deirdre's were standing around them, looking at the scene, too. For one moment, for the smallest of moments, Till tried to feel like Christmas, tried to hold on to the flap of the angel's wings and the silver glow of the star.

But then the manger scene began to move, too, Joseph standing up and stomping, others who were related to the participants beginning to talk in normal voices and laugh, the angel scrambling down off the roof.

And one of the wise men and one of the shepherds broke rank, and walked toward them.

The shepherd reached them first.

"It is *you*," said Till. "Melanie! I knew it."

"I had to do it," said Melanie. "I couldn't help it. What are *you* doing here?"

"Had to? Had to?" said Till.

114

Melanie reached up and pushed back the shepherd's headdress tied around her head. Light glinted off her earlobes.

"That was the deal to get my ears pierced. It was a trade-off. I *knew* someone would see me."

"What are you *wearing* under that bathrobe?" asked Till nastily.

Melanie looked down as if to check, then said, "Clothes, I'm wearing clothes!"

"Show me," said Till.

She waited. Deirdre waited. Melanie waited.

Melanie broke. "Well, long underwear, and my mother's old wool pants and a sweater . . . Till, you won't tell anybody, will you?"

The music of the carols and the Beatles and maybe even the Grateful Dead resounded in Till's head. Revenge would be sweet.

But maybe the flap of the angel's wing had brushed over her after all. She studied Melanie, making her squirm, watching her hand creep up toward the shepherd's headdress and fiddle with it.

Then she said, "Why should I?"

Her eyes met Melanie's, and a phrase of Till's father sprang unbidden to her lips. "Anyway, a hundred years from now, who'll know the difference?"

"Oh," said Melanie, uncertainly.

"Melanie!" A figure near the church hall entrance was waving.

"That's my mom." Melanie looked at Till a moment longer.

"Merry Christmas," said Till, enjoying herself.

"Yeah," said Melanie. Clutching her bathrobe tightly around her, she hurried away.

"Mrs. Gladiolus." Till heard her mother's voice, and they all turned and saw Till's mother, who only a little while before had been playing air guitar and singing Beatles' songs, now standing stiff as one of the angels.

"We do appreciate your letting your son participate in our celebration of Christmas," said Mrs. Gladiolus, smiling beneath the black mustache and pointed beard glued to her upper lip and chin.

"Thank Samuel," said Mrs. Wyndham. She gave Samuel a little nudge.

"Oh. Thank you, Samuel," said Mrs. Gladiolus.

"You're welcome," said Samuel proudly.

Then Annabel, who'd been studying Mrs. Gladiolus with a puzzled frown, said loud and clear, "Can women be wise men in *your* church?"

Everyone froze. Mrs. Gladiolus looked down at Annabel, and then back up at everyone. "Why, yes, dear."

"Out of the mouths of babes," said Mr. Wyndham.

Annabel took a deep breath. Everyone waited. But what she was going to say next was lost, for Mary had come up, holding Peter.

"Over to you Samuel," said his mother, and the moment passed.

Samuel reached out, and Mary put Peter into Samuel's arms.

Still puzzled, Mrs. Gladiolus said, "Won't you stay for some refreshments in the Church Hall?"

"We had some earlier, thank you. We need to get home," said Mrs. Wyndham.

She turned, then stopped. "Merry Christmas, Ms. Gladiolus," she said.

Mrs. Gladiolus smiled. "Merry Christmas," she said. "Mrs. Wyndham."

13

Upon a Midnight Clear

Till swallowed a yawn, and her ears popped. Christmas Eve was winding down. The stockings were hung by the chimney, one for everyone including all four parents, making the mantle look as if particularly fancy laundry had been put up to dry. Annabel and Samuel had just left a plate of cookies and a Coke on the end table nearest the Christmas tree, and gone reluctantly to bed, where Peter, reswaddled in his pajamas, had long since been asleep. It was very late, nearly midnight.

Deirdre, sitting crosslegged by the tree, was idly

arranging and rearranging the battered figures in the old manger scene. She looked up and caught Till's eye, and they both looked away.

Around them, the conversation hurried on, dancing in and out among stories and laughter.

"Remember," said Leah Frances, "remember when you taped the hem of your skirt up *way* above your knees for the School Choral?"

Till stole a look at her Mom's corduroy-covered knees.

Till's mother shook her head, laughing.

"She did," Mrs. Frances went on. "The music teacher, Ms. Colqwait, a woman without a drop of music in her whole body, I might add, got up there and lifted her baton and then she *saw Susannah's knees*. This was back before miniskirts had even hit this part of the world."

Miniskirts? Mom? thought Till.

"And then she just stood there, holding that baton up, her mouth open . . . so finally, someone started singing, and then we all started, remember? And about eight bars later, Ms. Colqwait caught up. The whole school auditorium was laughing by then. . . ."

Mom? thought Till. Deirdre's mother looked more like someone who would do that. Someone extravagant, and full of edges. Not her mother, calm, considering.

Her father was laughing, Till noticed, leaning forward, cracking nuts and interrupting from time to time with stories, too. The dark look had gone from his face, and every once in awhile, he and Till's mother would look at each other and smile. Meanwhile, Deirdre's father, who had the place of honor, reclined in the recliner, listening, not saying much, his shoes off to reveal bright red socks.

I bet Deirdre's mother picked those out, thought Till suddenly.

The Seth Thomas clock on the mantel struck twelve.

Everyone seemed to become aware of Till and Deirdre at once.

"Time you girls were in bed," said Till's father.

"It's only midnight," said Deirdre. "I stay up much later than this all the time. Don't I, mother?"

"Well . . ." said Deirdre's mother. "Not exactly, Deedsy."

"How can Santa Claus come if you two don't go to bed?" said Susannah Wyndham.

"Mo-*ther!*" Till couldn't believe her ears.

"Santa Claus," said Deirdre at the same time, in tones of deepest disgust.

"Go on, then," said Deirdre's father, as unexpectedly as the striking of the clock, and another little silence fell, marched along by the clock's ticking.

Deirdre sighed, and slowly, deliberately, unfolded her legs and rose to her feet. With the same slow deliberation she leaned forward and kissed her mother's cheek, and then her father's. "Good-night, Mrs. Wyndham, good-night, Mr. Wyndham," she said.

Till scrambled up from her place on the rug by the fire, so no one would notice Deirdre had excluded her from the good-nights. " 'Night, Mom, Dad." Till copied Deirdre, sliding a kiss along her mother's cheek and then her father's. But she held her hand out formally to each of Deirdre's parents as she said good-night to them. She could feel Deirdre watching, although Deirdre had already turned away toward the door when Till was finished.

"Merry Christmas," said Till's mother, as Till followed Deirdre.

"Merry Christmas," echoed the others, and then picked up the thread of conversation again before Till was out of the room.

They got ready for bed in silence, not as uncomfortable as Till had expected it to be. In spite of wanting to stay up, of over and over again stretching her eyes as wide open as they would go, the weight of sleep was heavier and heavier on her eyelids. She was first into bed, and she was fast asleep before Deirdre even turned out the light. She didn't even have time to worry whether she should risk saying Merry Christmas to Deirdre, only to have the wish go unreturned.

She didn't know how long she slept. It felt like a long, long time, but a faint light under the door showed that lights in the house were still on, people were still up. She didn't know what woke her at first. Then she realized how still the room was. Deirdre's bed was empty.

She's run away! thought Till, bolting up in bed. She's run away, and it's all my fault. She turned on her bedside lamp with sweaty hands.

Deirdre's suitcase was still under the bed. But her robe and slippers were gone.

Stupid, thought Till. She just went to the bathroom. Till turned the light off and lay back down, and waited for her heart to stop its panicky pounding and for Deirdre to come back.

She waited and waited. Her heartbeat returned to normal, but Deirdre didn't return.

At last Till got up and slid out into the hall. The bathroom door was open, the bathroom dark. Till made her way toward the kitchen, where the sound of voices was rising and falling now, with bubbles of soft laughter, as if the conversation were something being slowly cooked and stirred.

Till stopped, just out of reach of the rectangle of light coming through the slightly open kitchen door. The rectangle widened. Deirdre came out holding a glass of water. Hastily, Till stepped back. She didn't want Deirdre to think she was spying on her.

But the movement, the whisper of sound, made Deirdre look up. She peered into the dark hall and said, softly, "Who's there?"

"Me," said Till. "Just me."

"What are *you* doing?" Deirdre drew herself up and waited, warily.

"I woke up," Till whispered, and stopped as the murmur of voices picked up again. "You weren't there, and after awhile, I got worried. Sort of."

"Sure." Deirdre started forward again. "Fine."

And then through the door and down the hall came a burst of laughter, and Deirdre's mother's voice. "Isn't she funny. Twelve going on forty, I tell you."

Deirdre and Till both froze as the voice went on. "Such mannerisms. That bathrobe with those initials. So *forties*. But, Susannah, I swear, I don't know how I got such a rules-and-regulations Miss Priss for a daughter. She's like something out of Jane Austen, one of those characters with no sense of humor and full of prickles. It's almost impossible not to laugh at her sometimes. Which in her book is the worse sin of all!"

"Ohhhh." Deirdre said the word so softly that Till almost didn't hear it.

"Deirdre," said Till urgently. But before she could get any further, her own mother's voice came to them out of the general laughter.

"I know exactly what you mean, Leah. Matilda is now Till. Nothing babyish for her anymore. I expect she practices writing her name in a thousand different ways inside her notebooks. And you should have seen all the rigamarole she wanted for Christmas. She thought because it was in a magazine, it must be the end all and be all of sophistication . . . artificial trees decorated with color-coordinated ribbons. Roast goose!"

"Oh!" said Till, forgetting to keep her voice down.

"Such cute babies," said Leah Frances. "Were we ever that young?"

"And you know what she always says," said Susannah Wyndham.

"Let me guess," said Leah.

Together, the two mothers chorused, "*Mo*ther!" and the sound of all four parents laughing together broke like a tidal wave over the two girls standing in the hall in the dark.

Deirdre made a motion toward the kitchen door, as if she would storm the kitchen. Till grabbed her arm, hardly knowing what she was doing.

"No," she hissed. Deirdre stopped, swung back around to Till, her eyes staring. Then she dropped the glass and fled. Till stood for a moment, watching the pool of water spread out on the rug. Then she bent and picked up the glass, hoping numbly that the hall carpet would absorb all the water and no one would notice, and followed Deirdre.

Now Deirdre's suitcase was on the bed. She was snatching at things furiously in the dark. "I hate her, I hate her. I hate them. How *dare* they . . ."

Till stumbled over to her own bed and dropped down on it, still holding the glass. Realizing it, she put the glass carefully down on her bedside table, and turned on the lamp.

"I hate her, I hate her . . ." Deirdre kept on jamming things into her suitcase, her back to Till.

"Deirdre," said Till.

Deirdre ignored her.

"Deirdre, what are you doing?"

Then Deirdre turned to face Till, tears streaking down her cheeks, her eyes narrow and glittering. "What does it look like I'm doing, stupid!"

"Stupid! Stupid?" Something in Till gave way all at once. Scalding words burned her tongue for a moment, and then she was flying up off the bed, her arms flailing, the words boiling out of her. "Who are you calling stupid? You're the stupid one! Miss Priss!"

"Don't you dare!"

"Dare!" said Till. "Priss, priss, priss."

"You! Roast goose! Hah to you. You wouldn't know sophisticated if it came up and bit you on the knee."

"Well . . . well, that's about how sophisticated you are, about up to your knees. What a show-off! What a snob. No wonder people laugh at you!"

"Oh, yeah?"

"Yeah! You're . . . you're no better than the rest of us!"

"Who said I was? You're the one who kept expecting me to act like, like some movie star. You're the one who kept wanting to hear about New York, like I was somebody from another planet! You're the one who acts so cool — Matilda Wonderwoodswoman!"

"Oh, yeah? Oh yeah . . ." Till's voice trailed off, hearing her mother's words again. She looked at Deirdre.

"How could she?" said Till, her own eyes filling with tears. "How could my mother do that to me?"

Deirdre sat down. She looked at the bundle of underwear she was clutching, then reached over and dropped it back in the drawer.

"I hate them all," said Deirdre, in a conversational voice.

"Me, too," said Till. "I'll never ever ever forgive them."

From the hall came the sounds of voices, their parents going to bed for the night at last. Till roused herself enough to turn off the light. She and Deirdre sat silently in the dark, listening to the sounds of the house settling down, waiting for the house to grow quiet.

"How could they," said Deirdre, softly.

"It's like they went to evil mother school," said Till.

"Our fathers laughed, too," Deirdre pointed out.

"True."

Deirdre got up, closed the suitcase, and pushed it back, wadded clothes and all, under the bed. She lay down on top of the covers and folded her hands across her chest.

"If you were dead," volunteered Till, "they'd be sorry."

"Yes."

Till lay down, too.

"They were never our age," said Till. "They couldn't say those things if they had been."

"Agreed."

"Just because they said it, doesn't make it true."

There was a long pause. Then Deirdre said, an edge of animation in her voice, "True."

"They aren't always right, you know."

"True . . ."

Till and Deirdre lay still, as still as if they were much younger, listening for the sound of reindeer hooves on the roof.

Then Deirdre said, "You want . . . I mean, would you like to have a sleepover?"

Till said, slowly, "You mean in the living room? Now?"

"Yeah. Why not?"

"Why not?" agreed Till.

Quietly, carefully, not speaking another word, they gathered up their pillows and blankets. They sneaked down the hall and into the living room, where the banked fire still cast a pale glow from behind the firescreen.

The Coke and cookies still stood on the table.

"We'll catch him this time," whispered Till.

"We'll make him sorry he ever hit this house," Deirdre whispered back.

Feet to the fire, they settled in. Tilting her head back, Till caught the glint of firelight off her egg. Deirdre's, she knew, was still on the card table, now pushed into a corner of the room.

"Deirdre? You forgot your egg for Santa. And it's really good."

"Who cares," said Deirdre. "And don't patronize me!"

"You're a jerk," said Till, forgetting to keep her voice low.

"Shh!"

"A total nerd dweeb jerk," she grated out.

"Same to you, only more of it," Deirdre shot back.

They lay still in silence for a little while. Then Deirdre said, "I'm sorry."

Till thought about it. "If I say I'm sorry, are

you going to think I'm patronizing you?"

Deirdre didn't answer. Then, unexpectedly, Till heard a little snort, not at all delicate.

"Okay," she said. "Okay."

They lay still then, and after awhile, Till heard the even sound of Deirdre's breathing and knew she had fallen asleep.

It's Christmas day, Till thought. Someday, on Christmas day, I'll wake up and there will be snow all around, snow on the roof of my chalet in the mountains. And I'll have a fireplace in my bedroom, and a silk bathrobe, and someone will come in and light the fire, and hand me the bathrobe, when I wake up. Someday, on Christmas day, I'll wake up. . . .

14

Merry Christmas to All

Till woke up. The first thin gray light of morning was at the window. She forgot where she was, then remembered. Her feet were cold. The fire had long gone out. Deirdre was still asleep.

Wrapping her blanket like swaddling clothes around her, Till got to her knees and edged on over to the tree. She stretched and plugged in the lights.

She leaned back on her heels, and smiled a little. Put that in your egg, Mr. Fabergé, she thought.

Then a package caught her eye, a package with a card almost as big as the package itself taped to the outside. Till's first name was printed across the front in familiar handwriting.

Aunt Clare, thought Till. Mom and Dad must have put it here last night.

She picked it up. A book, that was easy enough to tell. By careful picking and persuading, she was able to work one end open.

It was a book, an old book. *My Antonia*. Willa Cather.

Till frowned, then opened the card. Inside she read:

Till — Willa Cather did a good part of her growing up in Nebraska, then left and lived in a lot of different places — including New York. She wrote one of her best books, if not her best, about one of the places she left behind.

Love,
Clare

For a little while longer, Till sat, holding the book balanced in both hands. But the light was growing golden outside. And Deirdre had turned over and begun to burrow deeper into her covers.

Quickly, carefully, Till put the book back where she could unwrap it again first thing. Then she shuffled back to Deirdre.

One of Deirdre's feet slid out from her cocoon

of blankets, and Till saw that she was still wearing her bedroom slippers.

It figures, Till thought. She smiled. "Deedsy."

Deirdre said, without opening her eyes, "If you ever call me that again, I will personally kill you."

"Deirdre, it's Christmas."

Frowning, Deirdre opened her eyes. "I hate Christmas."

"I do, too," said Till.

Deirdre yawned. "They can have it."

"You know what?" asked Till. "It doesn't matter. It's just one kind of Christmas. Theirs. Their own stupid old Christmas. But it doesn't have to be ours. When we get a little older, we can do whatever we want."

Deirdre was quiet. Then a little smile curled her lips.

"Roast goose," she said softly.

Till smiled, just a little, back. "Exactly," she said.

"Or something vegetarian, maybe."

"To match the tree," said Till. "Who knows."

The light thinned from gray to gold. Till heard the door of Annabel's room thump open. Almost immediately, she heard Samuel's door thump, too. Tandem footsteps thudded down the hall towards Till's parents' bedroom.

"It's Christmas," said Till.

"Mmm."

"And not all of it's bad. They're just parents,

132

you know. They can't help it they're not perfect or anything."

"They're not perfect. This is true. Unfair, but true."

"It *is* Christmas, no matter what people do." Till freed one arm from her blanket and gestured. The cookies were gone, and most of the Coke. The stockings were bulging. "Look. Deirdre."

Deirdre sat up.

"Santa's been here," said Till. "That proves it."

"He forgot the egg." Deirdre stood, and went over and got the Christmas egg she'd made for Santa.

"He's not perfect, either," said Till.

"Well," said Deirdre. She looked the tree over, then reached up and hung the ornament carefully on the branch next to Till's sequined egg.

"There," she said. "When in Rome . . ."

"Or in New York," said Till.

"Or in Evergreen," said Deirdre.

The thunder of approaching families sounded in the hall.

"Merry Christmas, Till," said Deirdre.

"Merry Christmas, Deirdre," said Till. "Merry Christmas."

About the Author

Nola Thacker was born in Montgomery, Alabama, and lived in Tennessee, Ohio, and Nebraska. She is now settled in Brooklyn, New York, along with her two cats, Georgia Peach and Sadie Tomato, and her dog, Shug.

Ms. Thacker's first novel, *Summer Stories*, won the Alabama Library Association Award. *Till's Christmas* marks her Scholastic Hardcover debut.

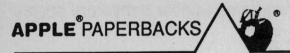

APPLE® PAPERBACKS

Pick an Apple and Polish Off Some Great Reading!

BEST-SELLING APPLE TITLES

❑ MT43944-8 **Afternoon of the Elves** Janet Taylor Lisle	$2.75
❑ MT43109-9 **Boys Are Yucko** Anna Grossnickle Hines	$2.95
❑ MT43473-X **The Broccoli Tapes** Jan Slepian	$2.95
❑ MT40961-1 **Chocolate Covered Ants** Stephen Manes	$2.95
❑ MT45436-6 **Cousins** Virginia Hamilton	$2.95
❑ MT44036-5 **George Washington's Socks** Elvira Woodruff	$2.95
❑ MT45244-4 **Ghost Cadet** Elaine Marie Alphin	$2.95
❑ MT44351-8 **Help! I'm a Prisoner in the Library** Eth Clifford	$2.95
❑ MT43618-X **Me and Katie (The Pest)** Ann M. Martin	$2.95
❑ MT43030-0 **Shoebag** Mary James	$2.95
❑ MT46075-7 **Sixth Grade Secrets** Louis Sachar	$2.95
❑ MT42882-9 **Sixth Grade Sleepover** Eve Bunting	$2.95
❑ MT41732-0 **Too Many Murphys** Colleen O'Shaughnessy McKenna	$2.95

Available wherever you buy books, or use this order form.

Scholastic Inc., P.O. Box 7502, 2931 East McCarty Street, Jefferson City, MO 65102

Please send me the books I have checked above. I am enclosing $_____ (please add $2.00 to cover shipping and handling). Send check or money order — no cash or C.O.D.s please.

Name_____ Birthdate_____

Address _____

City_____ State/Zip _____

Please allow four to six weeks for delivery. Offer good in the U.S.A. only. Sorry, mail orders are not available to residents of Canada. Prices subject to change.

APP693